Clover Twig
and the
Incredible
Flying Cottage

Clover Twig and the Incredible Flying Cottage

Kaye Umansky

Illustrated by Nick Price

First published in Great Britain in 2008 by Bloomsbury Publishing Plc
36 Soho Square, London, W1D 3QY

Text copyright © Kaye Umansky 2008
Illustrations copyright © Nick Price 2008

A CIP catalogue record of this book is available from the British Library

ISBN 978 0 7475 9063 7

All papers used by Bloomsbury Publishing are natural, recyclable products
made from wood grown in well-managed forests. The manufacturing processes
conform to the environmental regulations of the country of origin.

Typeset by Dorchester Typesetting Group Ltd
Printed in Great Britain by Clays Ltd, St Ives Plc

1 3 5 7 9 10 8 6 4 2

www.bloomsbury.com
www.kayeumansky.com

To Mo and Ella

Chapter One

Wanted. Storng Gril to Cleen

Clover Twig stood at the garden gate, staring in at the witch's cottage – and the cottage stared right back. The windows were like black eyes – small, dark and sunken. Ivy drooped over them like hooded eyelids.

The gate was secured with a loop of old string. Clover pulled it free, and gave a brisk push. The gate remained firmly closed. She pushed again.

The gate said, 'Take the hand off!'

The voice came from deep within the bars. It sounded bossy, like a guard in a museum who has spotted you blowing your nose on a priceless tapestry.

'What?' said Clover.

'Take the hand off!' This time the tetchy order was accompanied by a puff of rust, most of which showered down on to Clover's boots.

'Well, thanks for that,' said Clover. 'I polished those this morning.'

'The hand. Take it *off*. Then go away.'

Clover kept her hand right where it was. She wasn't about to be ordered around by an old gate, even if it did belong to a witch.

'I'm not going anywhere,' she said firmly. 'And I won't take my hand off until you give me a bit of service. How come you're able to talk, anyway?'

'How should I know? I'm a gate.'

'I suppose it's some kind of magic spell, is it?'

'Not my department. I open, I shut. That's it.'

Clover glanced up at the watchful windows. Behind one, she thought she saw a movement.

It's *her*, she thought. She's waiting in the dark behind the curtain. Waiting to see if I'm put off.

We will be spending some time with Clover, so let's look at her for a moment.

Tidy brown plaits. Steady blue eyes. Brown cloak, getting on the small side. Beneath the cloak, a green dress – faded, but clean and well pressed. Over her arm, a basket containing an apron. On her feet, patched old boots, polished as well as patched old boots can be. Altogether neat and respectable, which is how she always looks.

'Let me in,' she said. 'I'm here to see Mrs Eckles.'

'Name?' snapped the gate.

'Clover Twig.'

'Friend or foe?'

'Friend. But if I were a foe, I'd hardly be likely to say so, would I?'

'Oh *ho*! *Backchat* now. *That's* not going get you in, is it?'

'What is, then?' Clover was getting tired of standing around arguing with a gate. She gave it another shove.

'Just don't *push* me,' snapped the gate. 'Purpose of visit?'

'I'm here about the job.' Clover reached into her basket, produced an old envelope and held it up. 'See?'

On the back, in a spidery scrawl blissfully

untroubled by punctuation were the following
words:

> WANTed
> STOrNg gRIL To CLEEN aPPLy mRS
> ECkLES COTTaGE iN THE woods sicK
> PenS A wEEK bRiNG AN AYpRUN

Beneath was a small, rudimentary map, consisting of
scribbled lines, thumb marks and a lot of very badly
drawn trees. In the middle was what looked like a
toddler's attempt at drawing a house, together with
an arrow and the word **ME!**

Clover had spotted it the day before, pinned
crookedly on the village noticeboard.

It was the 'sick pens' that had caught her eye. Six
whole pennies! Most cleaning jobs didn't pay more
than four pence. It was too good to miss – although
she had a feeling that her mother would have something to say.

'Password?' rapped the gate.

'*Password?*'

'You heard.'

'I don't know anything about a password.'

'In that case,' sneered the gate with relish,
'Admittance Denied.'

Just at that moment a testy voice shouted, 'Is that gate givin' you grief?' It came from behind the front door.

'Yes,' called Clover. 'It's going on about a password.'

'Ah, it's just bein' difficult. Give it a kick.'

'With pleasure,' said Clover. And she drew back her foot and gave the gate a small, but very hard, kick. It slammed open in a furious squeal of hinges.

'Thank you so *very* much,' said Clover, and walked through with her nose in the air. Behind her there came a huffy crash, which she ignored.

And now she was in the witch's garden.

It wasn't a pretty sight. Thistles, nettles and weeds, jostling for space. A collapsed washing line. A crumbling well. An old bucket lying on its side in the mud, trailing a frayed bit of rope. An ancient water barrel, covered with green scum. It didn't bode well.

Clover stared up the path, giving the cottage her full attention. It was old. Very old. The thatch was going bald. The walls were held together by creepers and the whole structure sagged heavily to one side as though it was too exhausted to stand up straight. The angle of the twisty chimney was quite frightening. The windows still had that watchful air, like they were inspecting her. Giving her the once-over.

Clover didn't even blink. She was good at staring. She wasn't about to lose a staring match with a pile of old bricks. Not after coming all this way. Finding the cottage had taken for ever. It was well off the beaten track and the map was hopeless. But Clover had a stubborn streak. In the end, she had found it. Hidden in the deepest, darkest part of the forest, sitting plonk in the middle of a small clearing, encircled by a wildly overgrown hedge and protected by a talking gate.

The staring match was getting nowhere, so Clover decided to call it a draw. She thrust the paper into her pocket and crunched up to the flaking front door, which unhelpfully lacked a knob, handle, knocker or bell. She gave a brisk knock.

'I'm here,' she called, half expecting the door to talk back to her.

Silence. Clover waited, straightening a crease in her old green dress. She would have liked to have worn her better blue one, but it was torn. Sorrel, of course — the youngest of her three sisters. She coveted Clover's blue dress and was always sneakily trying it on.

Clover rapped again.

'Mrs Eckles? Are you there?'

She pressed her ear to the rough wood. Instantly,

there was a strange, unpleasant *tingling* sensation. Before she could jerk her head away, the testy voice spoke directly into her ear.

'What you usin' this door for? It don't open. Sealed up with a protection spell. Go round the back. Left, past the privy, round the log pile.'

Round the back was a big surprise. The front was dark and unwelcoming, but the back was very different. For a start, it was bathed in sunshine. Like the front, the back wall of the cottage was covered with a thick, ancient growth of ivy, but here it looked charming rather than sinister. A robin perched on one of the tendrils, singing its heart out.

There was a herb bed, a bird bath and a patch of lawn, where two plump chickens strolled around searching for worms. There were flowers that didn't appear to pay any attention to seasonal rules. Bluebells, lavender and roses were all in bloom at the same time. An ancient, sun-bleached bench was set at the far end, in the sunniest spot.

Best of all, in the middle of the lawn grew a cherry tree. It was covered in pink blossom. A bird feeder hung on the lowest branch.

'Admirin' me tree?' said the voice from the doorway.

So. This was the witch.

Clover had seen her from time to time, but usually in the distance, hobbling away from the village shop, whacking stray dogs and small children out of her way with a stick. She didn't seem very sociable. She never stopped to talk or gossip. She always wore the same clothes – an old black cloak, button boots and, when it was raining, the traditional pointy hat. This was the first time that Clover had seen her close up.

She certainly looked the part. She had the hooked nose, the pointed chin and the mad grey hair. No warts – but people said warts were optional, like the extra finger. Clover did a quick finger count and was relieved to discover that she had the normal amount.

But she had witchy eyes. Sharp, knowing, emerald green ones that didn't miss much.

'I were a girl when I planted that,' said Mrs Eckles. 'Did it with me sister. Fought like blue blazes, 'cos there was only the one spade. A wonder it survived. All them lightning bolts. All them sparks flyin' around. All that smoke.'

'Goodness,' said Clover. 'It sounds like quite a row.'

'It was. We didn't mess about.' Mrs Eckles folded her arms and looked Clover up and down. 'I knows you. You're that young Clover Twig. Yer pa calls 'imself a woodcutter. Spends all his time in The Crossed Axes.'

'It's thirsty work,' said Clover. 'His back's playing up.'

'Yes, well, he's yer pa, you would stick up for 'im. Yer ma's got 'er 'ands full. Too many kids to feed. You're the eldest. You'll be eleven next birthday.'

'Yes,' said Clover, surprised. 'That's right.'

'You got three sisters an' one little brother. Fern, Bracken, Sorrel and Herbediah. Always wailin' for food.'

'That's true. But they won't be so hungry if I get the job.'

'Hmm. I dunno. I wanted strong. You don't look strong.'

'Stronger than I look.'

'Well, you gave that gate a good kick, I'll say that. But can you lift, unaided, all by yerself, a large double wardrobe?'

'I've never tried. Why, do you want one shifting?'

'No, but I might one day. Does yer ma know you're 'ere?'

'No,' admitted Clover. 'I thought I'd give her a surprise.'

She moved towards the doorstep and was just about to step up when Mrs Eckles said, 'That's far enough.' She was staring hard and tapping her chin with a gnarled finger.

'What?' said Clover. 'Are we waiting for something?'

'I'm decidin' whether to invite you over the threshold. I don't let any old rough riff-raff in. Could be thieves, con men, anything.'

'I'm not riff-raff,' said Clover.

'Plain old nosy parkers, then. No one comes in without an invitation. Place is all wired up with protection spells. Doorway, windows, chimney, all entry points covered. 'Specially the threshold. Used a double strength one, it's a killer.'

'So what would happen if I just walked in?'

'Try it and see. Mind yerself, though. Just stick yer hand out and use the tip of yer finger.'

Clover leaned over the doorstep and cautiously extended a finger into the dark doorway. There was an instant horrible, tingling, buzzing sensation, which crackled up her arm in a very unpleasant manner.

Hastily, she snatched it back.

'Effective, ain't it?' said Mrs Eckles cheerfully. 'Sorry, but you did ask. Anyway, you can come in now. I'm extendin' you an official invitation.'

'You are?' said Clover doubtfully, sucking her

finger, which was developing a small, painful blister.

'Yep. In you come, nothing'll 'appen. Not once you been properly introduced. Cottage, Clover Twig. Clover Twig, cottage. That's it, formalities over. Come on, come on, I won't eat yer.'

Chapter Two

First Off, Are You Stupid?

There was only one room downstairs, and it was in turmoil. Crockery was piled high in the sink and the stove was littered with blackened pans. All kinds of rubbish was dumped on the table: a mouldy turnip, a pestle and mortar, an old bird's nest, an axe, a single muddy boot and a plate containing the remains of cold scrambled eggs unattractively garnished with a sock. Two rickety chairs were piled high with old newspapers. The only place to sit was in the rocking chair, if you first removed the exploding bag of lurid green wool and the knitting needles.

There was a nasty, charred, burning smell in the air.

'I got a bit behind,' announced Mrs Eckles, casually waving her hand at the appalling mess as though it were a case of a few crumbs on the carpet. 'Me knees is playin' up. Run out o' cups, so don't expect tea.'

'I see you have a cat,' said Clover, nodding at the large, luxurious basket set beside the stove. It had a red cushion in it and was by far the nicest thing in the room. Beside it was a collection of lovingly arranged toys: a ball with a bell in it, a cork, a stuffed mouse, a selection of conkers and a piece of heavily chewed string.

'I 'ave,' said Mrs Eckles, sounding soppy. 'My Neville.'

'And that's his shrine, is it?'

'That's his *corner,* if that's what you mean. He ain't been in it lately. Gone off on one of his rambles. I bin out shoutin' an' rattlin' his biscuit tin, but no luck.'

'What's that burning smell?' asked Clover, sniffing.

'His fish. Bit of a crisis earlier. Forgot I'd put it on.'

'You want to be careful,' said Clover. 'The place could catch fire. Old cottages like this go up easily.'

'Dunno about *easily*,' said Mrs Eckles. 'But you're right, they do go up.'

'Anyway,' said Clover, beginning to unfasten her cloak, 'anyway, I'll make a start on the washing-up, shall I? Where do you keep the kettle?'

'Ain't said you've got the job yet. I only stuck the notice up yesterday. There might be a huge queue o' lasses later. Bigger ones. *Stronger* ones.'

'I'm first, though,' pointed out Clover. 'That shows I'm keen.'

'True. An' you didn't let the gate put you off, you gets points for that. But I needs to interview you in a proper manner. Ask you questions. I got 'em written down somewhere. You've caught me on the 'op, you 'ave.' Mrs Eckles began rummaging around in the chaos, picking things up and slamming them down, on a quest for the missing list.

Clover stared around the squalid kitchen, taking it all in. The grandfather clock with a slow, faintly sinister tick; the pointy hat, hanging from a hook on the door, along with a black cloak; the cauldron in the fireplace; the bunches of unidentifiable herbs hanging from the low rafters; the broomstick which, judging by the cobwebs, hadn't been used in a while.

Another low, partly open door revealed a narrow flight of twisty stairs leading up into darkness. Clover wondered what was up there.

'Hah! 'Ere it is, in the teapot.' Triumphantly Mrs Eckles waved another old envelope. 'Right. First off, are you stupid?'

'I don't think so. I know my letters and can count up to a hundred. But mostly, I'm good with a mop and bucket. That's what you want, isn't it?'

'Just yes or no will do. Can you cook?'

'Of course. Who can't?'

'Some can't. Some can. Some say they can't and can an' some say they can and can't.'

'Well, I can,' said Clover firmly.

'Got an apron?'

'Yes.' Clover held out her basket. 'Here it is, look, with little flowers on.'

'Got an attitude?'

'Pardon?'

'You heard. 'Ave you got an attitude? Because I don't like girls with attitude. I likes 'em respectful. I deserves a bit o' respect in me old age.'

Clover thought about this. Did she have an attitude?

'Well,' she said honestly, 'I do tend to say what I think.'

'Nothin' wrong with that. It's the way you says it. I can't be doin' with sulks and flounces and whinin'.'

'I don't think I do any of those.'

'Good. Green-fingered?'

'So-so. Not as good as Ma, but I usually remember to water –'

'All right, all right, next question.' Mrs Eckles peered at the list. 'Ah, yes, proud of this one. Describe yourself in five well chosen words.'

Clover thought.

'Hard-working,' she said. 'Tidy. Honest. Mostly sensible. And – sometimes stubborn.'

'That's eight,' said Mrs Eckles. 'I asked for five. Thought you said you could count. Never mind, never mind, it's a good enough answer. But a bit dull. I 'ope you got other things about you. I 'ope you got a sense o' fun. Know any jokes?'

'No.'

'Dance? Sing? Whistle while you work?'

'No. I'm not Snow White, you know.'

'Just as well, she'd get on yer nerves after a while. Too busy larkin' around to pay proper attention to security. What *can* you do that's entertainin'? Come on, come on, everyone's got a party piece.'

Clover thought. What could she do?

'Well,' she said, 'I'm quite good at staring. I can do it for ages, without blinking.'

'Go on then.'

Obediently, Clover fixed her steady blue eyes on a distant cobweb hanging from a rafter and stared. It was quite easy. She had a technique for it. Basically, she just went off into a pleasant little trance. Sort of retired into her head and thought about something else entirely, leaving her eyes to get on with it. It didn't matter what she thought about. It could be anything. Sometimes she emptied her mind and thought about nothing at all. That was quite restful.

After a minute or so, Mrs Eckles began tapping her foot.

'All right, that'll do. Not exactly earth-shatterin', is it? When I stare at things, they *do* summat. Prepared to live in?'

That came as a shock. Clover hadn't even thought about living in.

'You gets yer own room,' went on Mrs Eckles. 'In the loft. There's a bed.'

Ah. Now, that was different. At home, Clover shared a bed with her sisters. She couldn't imagine

the luxury of waking without someone's elbow in her ear.

'Well,' she said, 'I'll certainly give it a try.'

'Of course, we'd need to see 'ow we get on,' said Mrs Eckles. 'See if we suit each other.'

'Of course. And I'll need to take every Sunday off to visit home.'

'Fair enough. And you're 'appy with the terms? There's other stuff needs doin'. Shoppin', cookin', collectin' the eggs from Flo and Doris. That's the chickens. They takes turns. Flo does brown, Doris does speckled. You up for that?'

'Of course.'

'Last question,' said Mrs Eckles. Her eyes narrowed and her voice took on dark overtones. ''Ave you, or anyone in the family, got certain – shall we say – *Powers*?'

'Well, I've seen Pa lift up a pig with one hand. We think that's what put his back out. It was a very big pig, you see, and –'

'Nah, nah!' Mrs Eckles waved her quiet. 'I ain't talkin' about *pig*-liftin'. I means – *unusual* Powers? You know. Fortune-tellin'. Premonitions. Able to shift things about usin' the *Power o' the Mind*.' She gave a slow, meaningful wink. 'Like this,' she said.

Her green eyes swivelled to an old watering can

that stood by the back door.

To Clover's astonishment, the can began to rock. Gently at first, then faster. Then it swivelled on its base. Leading with its spout, rolling drunkenly from side to side like an old sailor, it propelled itself through the door. It hopped down on to the doorstep, then down again and out into the sunny garden, where it proceeded to water a clump of bluebells.

'Now, *that's* starin',' said Mrs Eckles. Her eyes were on Clover. She was clearly waiting for some sort of reaction. 'Can *you* do stuff like that?'

'No,' said Clover slowly. 'None of us can do stuff like that. We're not a – magical family.'

'Does it bother you? Stuff like that?'

'Well, I'm not easily rattled, if that's what you're getting at.'

'Ah,' said Mrs Eckles. 'Ah, but can you keep yer mouth shut? I don't want you snoopin' an' spyin' an' spreadin' gossip. Too many blabbermouths around. *All right, pack it in now, no need to drown 'em!'*

That was to the watering can, which immediately stopped watering and plonked down next to the bluebells.

'I'm here to clean,' said Clover. 'I don't pry and I never gossip.'

'In that case, I'll give you a trial. Work 'ere today and we'll see how you gets on. Scrubbin' brush under the sink, bucket in the towel cupboard, kettle's somewhere, I dunno, you'll 'ave to look. I gotta do me outside chores. Gotta oil that flippin' gate, put it in a better temper. Then I gotta look fer Neville. Can't do everything.'

''Course you can't,' said Clover, tying her apron strings and rolling up her sleeves. 'You leave me to it, and as soon as I've cleared a space, I'll make us both a nice cup of tea.'

Chapter Three

The Shoes Go First

We must leave Clover here. Someone else is demanding our attention.

Far, far away from the forest, in a mountainous region of high, jagged crags and blithering, icy winds, there is a castle. Castle Coldiron is its name. It stands right on top of the highest peak. It is all spires and pointy roofs and sharp bits. It looks dramatically impressive from a distance, but if you look closely, it is crumbling quite badly.

Here and there, sections of wall are missing. Bits of it have dropped off and plunged into the ravine far, far below, where a rough, raging river roars.

From the topmost turret window there is a good view of other lesser peaks. If you like rock and grey skies, this is the view for you.

The castle is home to another, very different witch. Her name is Mesmeranza and she has a Plan. It is an Evil Plan, full of sly cunning. If time, trouble and years of wicked brooding count for anything, it deserves to succeed.

Mezmeranza has a pale, heavily powdered face which at first glance looks quite young. But her eyes are older. They are emerald green and look like they've been around for a while. Her lips are painted red. Her black hair is swept up and secured with a scarlet comb. She is wearing a purple satin dressing robe and has matching high-heeled mules on her feet.

Currently, she is sitting in a high-backed chair next to the window, flipping through the pages of a shoe catalogue. Her nails are very red, very long and filed into points. Next to the chair is a polished glass table. On it sits a large glass ball. It is the size of a goldfish bowl. This is a Crystal Ball. Right now, it is nothing to get excited about, being filled rather boringly with drifting grey mist.

Mesmeranza's Plan requires quite a bit of multi-tasking, as Evil Plans so often do. As well as looking at shoes, she is in the middle of dictating a to-do list to a small, grey, frazzled-looking woman with flyaway hair, who is sitting at a desk some distance away, frantically scribbling into a little black book.

Behind the desk, two things are pinned to the oak-panelled wall. The first is a calendar, open to the month of May. Three days – the bank holiday – are circled in black. The words **THE PLAN!!!** are written inside, in bold black letters. Next to the calendar is a postcard of what could be a cottage. It is hard to tell, because it is a very small postcard pinned to the wall by a very large dagger.

The scribbler at the desk is Miss Fly. She has hollow cheeks, a long, red, stuffed-up nose and reddened eyelids. She has a liking for thick, wrinkled brown stockings and brown, shapeless cardigans covered in cat hairs. The pockets are full of screwed-up hankies. Miss Fly is a cat lover who is allergic to fur. Sad, really.

'What number are we on?' demanded Mesmeranza. Her sharp voice echoed across the room, causing Miss Fly to give a startled jump and drop her pencil.

'Five,' said Miss Fly nasally.

'I can't remember what I've said now. Read them out.'

Miss Fly gave a little sneeze, mopped her nose and began to read.

'Nubber One. Cottage. Nubber Two. Cake. Nubber Three –'

'*Number*,' corrected Mesmeranza. 'It's *Number*, not *nubber*. Speak properly.'

'Sorry, it's by Ebs.'

'What? Oh, your *Ems*.'

'Yes. It's by allergy.'

'Get rid of the mogs, then. Or, as *you* would say, bogs. Don't expect sympathy. Carry on.'

'Nubber Three. Disguise. Nubber Four. Boy. Nubber Five. Shoes.'

'Put the shoes first.'

'What?'

'The shoes go first. Before anything else, I need the right shoes. These red ones.'

Mesmeranza stabbed at a page with a crimson talon. The shoes she was pointing at were bright red, pointy and strappy, with perilously high heels.

'Haven't you got enough shoes?' ventured Miss

Fly, who went in for sensible, brown, wide-fitting flatties.

'No,' said Mesmeranza firmly. 'Shoes are vitally important. What have I always said, Fly? Get the shoes right, and everything else follows smoothly. We don't all go round with Yeti feet like you. So the list now reads: Shoes, Cake, Disguise, Boy.'

Miss Fly began worriedly crossing things out. 'So where do I put Cottage?'

'At the very end. The cottage will be the culmination of everything else.'

'So it's at Nubber Five now?'

'No. I haven't finished. *Number* Five, notice how clearly I say that, *Nummmber* Five is Find Hypnospecs. They'll be up in the attic, in amongst Grandmother's things in one of the old chests. I shall need them when I interrogate the boy. They haven't been used for years. I'll try them out on a footman, just to be sure they're working properly.'

'You can't do that,' said Miss Fly. 'You can't hypnotise the footben.'

'Yes, I can. I can do what I like. I'll choose an old doddery one, so it won't matter if something goes wrong. I must have the Hypnospecs. They're vitally important to the Plan.'

'How do they fit in again?' asked Miss Fly.

'Don't you *listen*? I've told you a million times.'

'I've forgotten. You've had so benny plans, I get confused.'

'I don't know why, it's very simple. Wearing a brilliant disguise, I come upon the boy unexpectedly in the woods. I befriend him, pick his brains of useful information, then use the Hypnospecs to wipe his memory. That's it. On to the next phase.'

'Have you decided on the disguise?' enquired Miss Fly.

'Ah. Now, I've given that a lot of thought. I'm still debating. It's essential he doesn't recognise me from the last time, when I was the old tomato-seller. What a sight I looked. I borrowed your shoes, remember?'

'Yes,' said Miss Fly shortly.

'That was the finishing touch, your shoes. My, did I look frumpy.'

'They're very cubfortable,' Miss Fly told her, 'by shoes.'

'Comfortable,' agreed Mesmeranza, 'but hideous. This time I'm thinking upmarket. I'm thinking Rich Lady Lost In The Forest. Different clothes, different voice, better shoes. And I shall wear Grandmother's Hat of Shadows, just to be on the safe side. I think that's up in the attic too. It's a filthy tip, I hope you've got overalls.'

'*Be?*'

'Yes, you. You don't expect *me* to go rummaging around up there, do you? That's one of your jobs, along with ordering the next cake. Tell Mrs Chunk to make it a chocolate one this time, it's good to have variety. Write it down, then. Why aren't you writing it down?'

'I'b just thinking.'

'Well, don't. *I* do the thinking round here. I come up with the ideas.'

'But I'b just thinking. The poisoned tobato didn't work, did it?'

'I'm very aware that the tomato was a slight error of judgement.' Mesmeranza gave a scowl. 'You'll notice I'm not repeating it. Anyway, how was I to know the wretched boy didn't like tomatoes? Stop raking over old history and write down cake.'

'But I was just thinking. Shouldn't it be sweets?'

'What?'

'Sweets are traditional.'

'Far too obvious. Sweets, gingerbread, apples, poisoned combs – they've been done to death. Cake is new. It has a wholesome, innocent quality. Nobody suspects cake.'

'Not everybody likes cake, though,' observed Miss Fly.

'Demelza does. I've already left three on her doorstep. She chomped through those happily enough.'

'But it's not her you have to convince, is it? It's the boy. Assubing he's looking after the cottage again, which you don't know, do you?'

'That's the whole point of *interrogating* him, Fly. I intend to find that out. Although no one else would feed that beastly cat and he's the only neighbour, so she's stuck with him. No, I'm positive it'll be the boy again.'

'The boy who wouldn't take the tobato.'

'Yes, *yes*! But I'm not *offering* him a tomato, am I? This time it's *cake*! He'll open the door and find a lovely, freshly baked cake sitting on the doorstep. A humble gift left by an anonymous admirer. Are you telling me he won't take it in? Especially if it's raining. No one leaves a cake out in the rain.'

'But how do you know it'll be raining?'

'I shall make it rain,' said Mesmeranza witheringly. 'I'm a witch. I can do that.'

'But he bight not be feeling like something sweet. He bight prefer a healthy alternative –'

'*He'll like cake!*' screeched Mesmeranza. Furiously, she slammed the catalogue shut. 'I've started now. I can't change tack in the middle, can I? Now I've established the idea of *cakes* appearing on the doorstep, like it's a normal thing. Don't you think it'd look suspicious if there was a – a box of *root vegetables* or something?'

'Better for you,' ventured Miss Fly, 'root vegetables.'

'*We're going with cake! Write it down!*'

Miss Fly wrote it down, sniffing sadly.

'Number Six,' went on Mesmeranza, 'Hair Appointment. I think I'll wear it up. I'll need to try it with the Hat. Actually, Hair should be Number Two. Or perhaps Three, after I've decided on the disguise. So it's One, Shoes, Two, Disguise, Three, Hair, Four, Cake, Five, Boy, Six, Hypnospecs, Seven, Hat. Although the Hat should really go with the disguise, which is Number Two. Number Seven –'

'Wait, wait, I can't keep up . . .'

'Number-Seven-Look-For-The-Bad-Weather-Umbrella-Number-Eight-Find-Grandmother's-Wand,' rattled off Mesmeranza, adding, 'Mind how you handle it. It might look harmless, but don't let it fool you. Latent magic build up, might take your hand off, which would be a waste of good power. Be careful of the Umbrella too, we don't want a flood.'

'Are you sure you should be using all that old equipbent?' asked Miss Fly doubtfully. 'It sounds . . . dangerous.'

'Of course it's dangerous! That's the whole point of it. Dark, dramatic and dangerous. That was Grandmother's style and it's mine too. I'm not messing about this time, Fly. I'm through with tomatoes. Demelza's been laughing at me too long. Slapping on more and more security spells. Flaunting her ownership. As if those crumbling old walls can keep me out.'

'They have so far,' pointed out Miss Fly.

'Not any more. This time I'm bringing out the heavy guns as well as doing a lot of careful planning, which brings me back to the list. Number Nine –'

'Wait a binute, wait a binute . . .'

'Number *Nine*, I've just remembered, I shall need Grandmother's Poncho of Imperceptibility.'

'Her *what*?'

'Poncho of Imperceptibility. She made it during one of her mad knitting periods. A nasty, lumpy, woolly thing with a hood. Anybody else would have stuck with a basic Cloak of Invisibility, but apparently ponchos were in at the time. Hardly a style statement, but it does the job. At least no one will see me.'

'No? Why is that?'

'Because it'll make me *vanish*, you fool. Anyway, it's in the attic somewhere. Find it.'

'Oh dear. All right. What colour is it?'

'It doesn't *have* a colour, Fly. It's *imperceptible*. You'll have to feel for it.'

'How do you know it's got a hood if you can't see it?'

'Because I tried it on when her back was turned. Right, I think that's everything. That leaves Cottage at Number Ten. Oh, and one last thing. Warn Chunk about the annual dungeon inspection.'

'Oh,' said Miss Fly pitifully. A strange expression came over her face. She groped for a hanky. 'Bust I?'

'Yes. It's long overdue. I've a feeling he's slacking. I think we've run out of prisoners, I've been too busy to even think about it. I don't want to find him gone off on one of his everlasting lunch breaks. What's the problem? Why are you looking like that?'

'No reason,' snuffled Miss Fly, who in fact had a very good reason for looking like that.

'Well, just make sure he's down there when I arrive. I hope the place is looking better than the last time. Stinking straw, doors wide open, rats everywhere. I had to *wade*. I don't think he ever lifts a finger. I'd fire him if it wasn't for his mother.'

'Perhaps you should anyway,' said Miss Fly hopefully.

'And lose Mrs Chunk? Are you mad? Anyway, that will be all. Take the list and copy it up in your best handwriting. Do it somewhere else, I can't stand your sniffing. Hurry up, I have things to do.'

'But I haven't quite –'

'Go! Now!'

Miss Fly hastily gathered up her hankies, her pencil and the little black book, and scuttled from the room.

The moment the door closed, Mesmeranza's emerald eyes went to the Crystal Ball on the glass table. She leaned down, picked it up and cradled it gently in her cold, white hands.

'Right,' she breathed. 'Time for a little peek.'

Miss Fly entered her apartment to a chorus of crazed howling. Her notebook flew out of her hand as a flurry of fluffy forms hurtled through the air and attached themselves to various bits of her with their claws.

More furry bodies swarmed up from ground level. A large tortoiseshell cat scrambled on to her shoulder and screamed in her ear. Three small kittens, silly with excitement, galloped up the curtains. A lean Siamese and a hefty black and white tom began circling their food bowls, tails shivering and mouths drooling in anticipation.

A small ginger cat crouched on the bed, enthusiastically coughing up a fur ball. A big cream-coloured one was sharpening his claws on the rug. A one-eyed grey began fighting with a small, ferocious-looking tabby.

'All right, darlings, in a binute, give be a bobent,' cried Miss Fly, sneezing, gasping, stumbling around, gently detaching the raking claws and fighting to get the screaming tortoiseshell's tail out of her face.

Her anxious eyes swept the floor. The litter boxes needed changing, she could see that, and someone had dragged fish bones all over the place, but that wasn't what she was looking for. Looking for, and dreading to find . . .

She saw it, just behind the door. Another note. The third in as many days. With a little gulp, she bent down, unfolded it with trembling fingers and read what it said.

'Oh dear,' sighed Miss Fly. 'Oh *dear.*'

Back in the turret room, Mesmeranza's green eyes

gazed down into the Crystal Ball. The swirling grey mist had disappeared. In its place a picture had formed.

A cottage. A small, ancient cottage in a tiny, sun-speckled garden. And in that garden, a girl in a green dress was standing beneath a miniature cherry tree, vigorously shaking out an old rug the size of a postage stamp. Tiny pink blossoms were floating down and landing in her hair.

'Hmm,' muttered Mesmeranza. She gave a frown. 'And who might *you* be, I wonder?'

As she watched, the girl spread the rug on the tiny lawn and walked back into the cottage, shutting the door behind her.

Mesmeranza waved a hand and the picture vanished in a grey swirl, sucked away just like water down the hole in a bath tub. Slowly, thoughtfully, she replaced the Ball on the table and sat back in her chair. This was new. This was something she hadn't bargained for. A strange girl. She would need to find out more. Tonight, hopefully, when she interrogated the boy.

But first things first.

Wincing a little, she eased off her high-heeled slippers, one at a time. For a long, blissful moment, she wiggled her newly freed toes.

Then she opened the catalogue to the right page, briskly tapped the relevant picture, clicked her fingers, stuck out her legs and waited for the new red shoes to arrive on her feet.

Chapter Four

I'll Have It!

'Where've you been?' cried Ma as Clover entered, bringing with her a blast of night air. 'It's nearly dark! Yer spud's in the oven, but it'll be all dried up by now.'

'I'll have it!' came the instant chorus from the table, where three small girls sat in a blizzard of paper, cutting out paper dolls.

'Covey!' shrieked Little Herby, hurling himself at Clover's knees. His head was sticky, as though it had been dunked in treacle.

'It's all right,' said Clover, hanging her cloak on the hook. 'I'm not hungry. I'll save it for breakfast. I've had some cake.'

She had, too. Mrs Eckles had unexpectedly produced it from a cupboard, to go with the tea. It was a rich, moist fruitcake, and together they had demolished the best part of it. Clover had eaten so much that in the end she had felt quite sick, and thoroughly enjoyed the novelty.

'*Cake?* Where'd you get cake from?'

'Got given it.'

'Lucky!' came the envious chorus from the table.

'Covey!' bellowed Herby again, clutching at her skirt, trying to climb up.

'Yes, Herby, it's me. Have you been a good boy?'

'Ess.'

'No, he ain't,' said Fern. 'Bracken put a pea up his nose and he wouldn't stop hollerin'.'

'Tattle tail,' said Bracken, pinching her sister's arm. Fern poked her with the sharp end of her scissors.

'See what I have to put up with?' said Ma wearily.

'What did you do to get it out?' asked Clover, picking up Herby and inspecting his nose, which did indeed look rather red.

'Poured honey up his nose,' said Sorrel, with a giggle. 'It went all in his hair. Ma made him sniff pepper and he sneezed it out.'

'They've been little monkeys all day, the lot of 'em!' cried Ma. 'You wait 'til yer pa gets home!'

'Aw, he won't do nuffin',' said Fern, with a shrug.

'Where is he? Down the tavern?' asked Clover.

'I reckon.' Ma gave a sigh. 'Sent him out to borrow a drop o' milk. That was an hour ago. His spud's in the oven an' all, turnin' black by now I shouldn't wonder.'

'I'll have it!' chimed in Fern, Bracken and Sorrel. There were never any leftovers in the Twig household.

'No, you won't, you've had yours,' said Ma.

'But we're still *hungry*,' whined Sorrel.

'Go to bed, then, and it'll soon be breakfast time. If there's any milk, that is.'

'Ma,' said Clover, dumping Herby on the floor. 'I've got some news.'

'You have? Like what?'

'I've got a job.'

'What? Stop *doing* that, you three.' Fern, Bracken and Sorrel were kicking each other's legs under the table. 'What job?'

'Cleaning. It's for Mrs Eckles.'

'What . . . the *witch*?' Ma's jaw dropped in shock. The girls gave a united gasp and sat bolt upright, eyes on stalks.

'Yes.' Clover picked up the broom and began sweeping up bits of paper.

'You've been to that *cottage in the woods*? On yer *own*? What were you *thinkin'*?'

'It's six pence a week, Ma. Five for you and one for me. Think of that.'

'Six?' Ma sounded thoughtful. 'Well, it's good wages, I'll say that.'

'I'll bring it round every Sunday, regular. And she keeps chickens. She said she'd send round some eggs.'

'Why every Sunday?'

'Well, that's my day off. I'd be living in, you see.'

'What – *leaving home*?'

Ma sank on to the bench, weak at the knees.

Instantly, Sorrel said, 'Can I have your blue dress?'

'You know it makes sense, Ma,' went on Clover, ignoring the interruption. 'One less mouth to feed.'

'I dunno,' said Ma doubtfully. 'I dunno.'

'I get my own room. She showed it to me. It's under the roof and there's a bed in it.'

'*I* want me own room,' whined Bracken. 'Not just

an ol' curtain.'

Over in the fireplace, Herby was playing with the fire irons. Ma shot up from the bench and rushed over to stop him inserting the poker in his ear.

'I don't know how I'll cope, mind,' sniffed Ma. 'Run rings round me, they do. Who'll mind Herby when I'm gettin' supper? Stop *doing* that, you three.'

At the table, all three girls were pulling each other's hair.

'It'll be a better supper though, won't it? More to go round,' said Clover, going to fetch the little brush and pan.

'I think she should go,' said Fern immediately, and Bracken and Sorrel nodded their heads in un-sisterly fashion.

Sorrel said, '*Can* I have your blue dress?'

'No,' said Clover. 'I'll be taking it. I'm taking all my things. And I want a word with you about that later,' she added darkly.

'I dunno,' said Ma doubtfully. 'I dunno what yer pa'll say. Not when he hears it's Mrs Eckles. What's she like, anyway?'

'All right. She's got a cat, but it's gone missing. It's got a posh basket with a cushion.'

'What's the place like inside?'

'Don't ask.' Clover rolled her eyes to heaven. 'I'll soon get it sorted, though. The kitchen's looking better already. I think she was pleased. She said it made a change to drink tea out of a clean cup. That's when she brought out the cake.'

'You shouldn't eat in a witch's house!' scolded Ma. 'Everyone knows that. It gives 'em power over you. She could have put you under a spell. Turned you into a frog.'

'Do I look like I'm turning into a frog?' Clover held up her hand. 'See? No webbed fingers. Anyway, I start properly tomorrow. I'm getting up early, so I'd better go and pack.'

'I dunno,' fretted Ma. 'I dunno . . .'

Clover stood holding back the curtain of the small sleeping space she shared with her sisters. You could tell she hadn't been home all day. The straw mattress was all of a heap. Ragged clothes and tangled blankets lay all over the floor, together with her torn blue frock.

Determinedly, she waded into the chaos. Tidy up first – and then, pack.

Tidying took quite a time, but packing didn't. Into Clover's basket went a pair of heavily darned stockings, her spare pair of drawers, her old cotton nightdress, her comb, the green ribbon she'd got for her ninth birthday and the blue one she'd got for her tenth, her toothbrush, her face cloth, her sewing things and her pincushion.

That was it. She didn't have anything else, apart from the clothes she stood up in.

A short time later, as she sat on the edge of the neatly made bed, sewing up the blue dress, she heard the door slam and the sound of muffled conversation. Pa was back, then. There came heavy footsteps and he poked his head around the curtain.

'Yer ma says you got a job cleaning for old Mother Eckles,' he said.

'That's right,' said Clover. 'It's six pence a week.'

'My little girl,' said Pa sentimentally. He wiped his eyes. 'Goin' off into the big, wide world.'

'It's only on the other side of the forest, Pa. I'll be back every Sunday.'

'Yer ma's worried. Thinks you'll get magicked or summat.'

'I'll be fine, Pa.'

'Ruben Barleymow showed me some stuff she gave him for his corns. Green ointment, it were.'

'Did it work?'

'I dunno. His wife wouldn't let him use it.'

'Well, that was silly, wasn't it? Now we'll never know.'

'She can read the tea leaves an' all,' went on Pa. 'Tilly Adams what serves down The Axes went an' had it done. Told her she'd meet a dark-'aired stranger who'd sweep her up orf her feet.'

'And did she?'

'Well, Tobe Thomas hoisted her up to the top shelf the other night so's she could fetch down a jar o' pickles.'

'Tobe Thomas isn't a stranger.' Clover bit off the thread with her teeth. 'And he hasn't got any hair, except what grows out of his ears.'

'Still,' said Pa. 'She got swept up. Um – did anything strange happen while you were there? Any – you know – *magical* goin's-on?'

Clover thought about the talking gate and the watering can that moved by itself. The tingling front door that wouldn't open because it had a spell on it. What had happened to her finger when she stuck it over the threshold. The way the cottage . . . stared.

'Not really,' she said.

'Aye. Well, you're sensible. You can always come home if you don't like it. But you watch out for yerself.'

'I will, Pa.'

'We'll miss you, though.'

'And I'll miss you, Pa.'

Clover jumped up and planted a kiss on his stubbly cheek. He smelled of ale.

Chapter Five

They Remind Me of Eyeballs

The evening shadows were lengthening as Wilf trudged along the forest track. He'd done four deliveries that day, all miles apart, and had a lot of injuries to show for his efforts. He had scraped knees (falling down a quarry), a bump on his head (walking into a tree), a throbbing ankle (missed his footing when crossing a stream) and squelchy socks (stepping into a bog). He would be glad to get home.

Wilf walked this path every evening on his way home. He knew every twist and turn. Every low branch, every root, every ditch. Well, he ought to. He'd banged into them, tripped over them and fallen down them enough times. He and the path home had a long, painful history.

On he trudged, keeping his eyes to the ground in case someone had dug a new hole for him to fall down while his back was turned. It wouldn't be long now before he reached the turn-off. Then, in no time at all, he would be back at the shack where Grampy would be cooking turnip stew for supper.

Wilf's stomach growled at the thought. Delivering other people's groceries always left him starving. Even worse was hanging around in the village shop, trying not to weep as the ancient proprietor, Old Trowzer, weighed and measured and filled the boxes with all manner of good things: currants, buns, apple pies, sugar lumps, jars of honey and sometimes – oh, the wonder of them! – fancy cakes. There were other items as well, but it was the cakes that got Wilf slavering.

He rounded the bend and pulled up short, with a little grunt of surprise. A figure stood before him, slap bang in the middle of the trail.

It was a woman. A tall woman, made even taller because she was wearing a pair of very red, very high, very spiky heeled shoes. She wore a black velvet cape which ended at the ankles. On her head was a wide-brimmed, floppy hat. It cast a dark shadow over the upper half of her face. All you could see was her mouth, which was a crimson slash.

This woman was rich, you could tell. She had jewelled rings on her red-tipped fingers. Fingers that looked as if they did nothing but snap to summon servants or tap in a bored way on long, polished tables. She looked like she could afford to buy all the fancy cakes in the world, if she wanted.

She looked ludicrously out of place in the forest.

'At last!' cried the strange woman. 'At long last, someone to help me!'

There was something about her voice Wilf thought he recognised. But that couldn't be, could it? She was a stranger. Occasionally, strangers might stop briefly at the village shop to buy a bun or ask the way. But they didn't look like this.

'Are you lost?' asked Wilf. He couldn't stop staring at her shoes. They were the sort of shoes that are unsuitable for anything – dancing, walking, even standing. Just looking at them made his eyes water.

'I certainly am. I've been blundering about *for ever.* I'm afraid I've had a bit of an accident.'

'Oh dear. You have?' Wilf knew all about accidents. He looked for the blood.

'Oh, nothing serious, although I believe I may have laddered my stocking.' The woman glanced down at her ankle and gave a rueful little laugh. 'I was on my way to a ball in town. I'm not exactly dressed for a walk in the woods.'

'But the nearest town's miles away.'

'I thought I'd take a short cut. And I have a very good, fast carriage. Well, I did until it threw a wheel some way back along the trail. So tiresome. I waited for *hours* in the hope someone would come along, but in the end I gave up. I set out hoping to find a wheelwright.'

'Piffle,' said Wilf.

'I beg your pardon?'

'Piffle. The next village on. They've got a wheelwright.'

'And how far is Piffle?'

'I dunno. Three miles?'

'Three *miles*?' wailed the woman. 'That far? I can't possibly walk three miles in these shoes. This is a disaster. Whatever shall I *do*?'

An awkward little silence fell. Wilf felt sure she

was waiting for him to offer to go for her. That would be the polite thing to do. But he couldn't. He didn't have it in him. His aches and pains were aching and paining. Supper called, and Grampy got grumpy if he was late. He had to get up at stupid o'clock in the morning. The wheelwright might be closed. It was getting dark. He just *couldn't*.

'Do you live nearby, boy?' enquired the woman.

'Not far,' said Wilf. 'At the next turn-off. It's just a shack in the woods.'

'How *quaint*. And do you live all alone?'

'With my grampy.'

'Hmm.' Thoughtfully, the woman tapped her chin with a beringed finger. 'Do you know, I've just had an *idea*. I could come along with you and wait in your little – *shack* – and you could pop along to Piffle and ask the man to come out. I'd pay you for your time, of course. Would two crowns be enough, do you think?'

Wilf's mouth fell open. Two crowns! *Two whole crowns!*

He would do it, of course. You don't turn down that kind of money. Grampy would make him any-way once he knew there was money in it. He would turn into a fawning heap once he found *that* out. He would put his teeth in and dust off the best chair and insist that Wilf set off right away. While he was gone, the strange woman would probably eat his share of stew.

'I've never been in a *shack*,' said the woman. 'What *fun*! And I'll bet Grampy's *adorable*.'

'I wouldn't say that, exactly,' said Wilf. 'But – well, all right, then. You'd better come along with me.'

'How kind,' said the woman. 'How *truly* kind.'

Together, they set off along the trail. Wilf kept darting sideways glances at his strange companion. Try as he could to see beneath the hat, her face remained in shadow. But there was something familiar about her, he was sure of it. He just couldn't quite put his finger on it.

'What's your name, dear?' asked the stranger, tucking her arm into his.

'Wilfred Brownswoody.'

'Tell me all about yourself, Master Brownswoody. How old are you?'

'I'm not sure. Twelve, I think. Grampy's a bit vague.' Politely, he tried to disengage his arm. There was something about her touch he didn't like. But the woman held on firmly.

'Doesn't your mother know?'

'I never got the chance to ask her. She and Dad went off to live in a caravan and dance in a travelling circus. They didn't take me because I couldn't get the hang of the tambourine.'

He always said it for a joke, although in fact it was near enough true.

'I imagine there are wolves in the forest,' said the stranger. She peered into the trees and gave a theatrical little shiver.

'I doubt it,' said Wilf. 'They stay away from this neck of the woods. They're scared of Neville.'

'Neville? And who is *Neville*?'

'A cat I know.'

'*Really?* You're a cat lover, then?'

'Nev's all right. Well, not to the wolves, obviously. I feed him sometimes, when Mrs Eckles is away.'

'Mrs *Eckles*. What jolly names you forest folk have. Who is this Mrs Eckles?'

'Our nearest neighbour.'

'And do you see a lot of her?'

'Not really.' Wilf wished she would stop holding his arm so tightly. Her long nails were digging into his wrist.

'Oh? Why is that?'

'She keeps herself to herself. She's the local witch.'

'*A witch? Really?* I imagined a plump, laughing country woman, with freckles. Mrs Eckles with jolly freckles, ha ha!'

'Ha ha,' agreed Wilf miserably. To his relief, she saw him wincing and relaxed her grip a little.

'So. What's she like? This Mrs Eckles?'

'All right,' said Wilf. 'I do a few jobs for her now and then.'

'Like what?'

'I used to chop her logs until she stopped me. I'm not too good around axes.'

'Anything else?'

'Last year I minded her cottage when she went off to the May Fayre at Palsworthy.'

'And will you be staying there again this year? The Fayre is coming up shortly, I believe.'

'I don't know. She hasn't asked.'

'No? She's made other arrangements? Someone to live in? A local, trustworthy girl, perhaps?'

'I doubt it. Most of the girls are afraid of her.'

'If there *was* such a girl,' mused the stranger, 'I expect she'd like *cake*, don't you?'

'Maybe,' said Wilf. 'I don't know.' It seemed a weird thing to ask. How was he to know whether girls liked cake? 'Anyway,' he added, 'Mrs Eckles is fussy about who she invites over the threshold. She doesn't trust many people.'

'But she trusts you.'

'Mmm. Sort of. It's just that it didn't work out too

well last time.'

'No? And why is that?'

'I broke a few things,' admitted Wilf glumly. 'Then there was the flood in the kitchen. And a small fire, though I managed to put that out.'

'Ah well. Accidents do happen.'

'They do to me,' agreed Wilf, adding, 'I didn't let anyone in, though. She can't blame that on me.'

'Good for you. Mind you, I don't suppose she gets many callers living around here. *Were* there any callers? While she was away?'

'Only one. Some old woman with a basket of tomatoes. Tried to get me to buy one, but I don't like tomatoes. They remind me of eyeballs.'

'I expect you like cake, though,' said the woman.

'I do,' agreed Wilf. 'Especially if it's got that white stuff on the top.'

'Sugar icing?'

'Yes. And a cherry in the middle. I delivered one once, and a bit sort of accidentally fell in my mouth.'

They had reached the turn-off.

'Oh dear,' said the woman, suddenly stopping and letting go of his arm. 'One moment. I think I have a stone in my shoe.'

She bent down and began fiddling with the strap.

'The shack's this way,' said Wilf, pointing. 'Only

another few minutes and we'll be there. It's a bit rough from now on. Perhaps it would be better if you took your shoes off altogether?'

He turned round. The woman had straightened up. Rather to his surprise, she had removed her hat. Instead, she was wearing an odd-looking pair of dark glasses, with green frames and thick lenses.

'Look into the glasses,' said the woman. Her voice had taken on a low, commanding quality. She moved towards him until they were almost nose to nose. 'Look deep. What do you see?'

Wilf stared. Deep within the lenses, he could see two little green sparks. They began to revolve.

'Little green sparks,' said Wilf. Or tried to. For some reason, his lips felt heavy and his tongue wouldn't move properly. 'Li'l . . . gree . . . spars. Yarp.'

'Are they spinning?'

'Mmmgh,' mumbled Wilf. 'Yarp.'

They were too. They made him feel dizzy, but for some reason he couldn't look away. Those madly revolving little green sparks seemed to be sucking all the thoughts from his head. He was feeling tired too. His eyelids felt really heavy. *Incredibly* heavy. The only way to stop the sparks spinning was to close his eyes . . .

From somewhere far away, yet at the same time

very close, he could hear the woman's voice.

'Feeling sleepy?'

'Yarp,' mumbled Wilf dreamily. 'Seepy, yarp.'

'You're under. Listen carefully. If you stay at the witch's cottage again, you will take the cake in, because you love cake and there is nothing suspicious, repeat, *nothing suspicious* about it. Do you understand?'

'Yarp.'

'Say it.'

'Nu'in' spishus 'bout cay.'

'Correct. I will count backwards from ten. When I snap my fingers, you will open your eyes, go straight home and forget everything about this meeting. You never saw me. Ten – nine – eight –'

Five minutes later, Wilf arrived home. He was rather surprised to find it considerably later than he thought. Grampy had the stew ready. It was turnip. It was a bit burnt. No surprises there. Rather like his day.

Chapter Six

So What's It Like in There?

It was the following morning and Clover was standing on one of the rickety chairs, leaning over the sink, washing the window which overlooked the sunny back garden.

'You're early,' said a voice from behind her. Mrs Eckles stood at the foot of the stairs, wrapped in an ancient dressing gown, feet stuffed into a pair of old carpet slippers, evidently just out of bed.

'It's almost noon,' said Clover. 'I've been here for hours.'

'No problems with the gate?'

'Nope. It's gone all smarmy. Said it hoped I'd have a nice day.'

'Aye. I oiled it. Give it a drop too much, I reckon.'

'Anyway,' said Clover, 'the back door was open, so I just came in and got started.'

'So I see. You're gettin' on.'

'I know,' said Clover cheerfully. 'I like a challenge.'

She had done a good job, she knew it. The kitchen was gleaming. She had scrubbed shelves, lined drawers, de-cobwebbed rafters, scraped out the cauldron and re-laid the fire with fresh kindling. She had washed the curtains and hung them out to dry. She had cleared out the pantry, throwing anything away that looked inedible, which was pretty well everything. She had scrubbed the flagstones, filled the oil lamps and replaced the wicks. She had set a jar of lavender in the middle of the table. And then she had made some biscuits, washing up as she went along.

She had thoroughly enjoyed herself. It was satisfying, bringing order out of chaos.

'I see you threw out me cherry jam.' Mrs Eckles

pointed at the big sack of rubbish standing by the door.

'I certainly did. It was all mouldy.'

'What am I s'posed to have for breakfast?'

'I've got some biscuits in the oven. They'll be ready in a minute.'

'Thought I smelled summat. Get the tea brewin' then, I could do with a cuppa.'

Clover gave the window a last brisk rub, jumped down and began setting out cups and saucers.

'Ooh,' said Mrs Eckles. ''Avin' it at the table, are we, in a proper manner? With the milk in a *milk jug*? There's fancy! And paper serviettes! Didn't know I 'ad any.'

'Buried under the old newspapers,' said Clover. 'They now live in the bottom drawer with the clothes pegs and the candles.'

'Forgot I 'ad a bottom drawer,' admitted Mrs Eckles. 'Can't stoop that far these days. With me knees.'

She hobbled to her armchair, picked up her wool bag, pulled out the green knitting, looked at it for a moment, sighed, then threw it on the floor.

'Not in the mood?' asked Clover.

'Not really. It's a new blanket for Neville.' Mrs Eckles cast a doleful look at the empty basket. 'I bin out searchin' the woods half the night. Left the back door open thinkin' he'd come in, but he ain't. You ain't seen him, I s'pose? On yer way over?'

'No. Of course, I don't know what he looks like.' Clover took the hissing kettle from the hob.

''Andsome,' said Mrs Eckles fondly. 'Black an' exceedin' 'andsome, with yeller eyes. Long whiskers. Bit missin' from one of his ears. Run-in with a wolf.'

'Sorry,' said Clover, pouring boiling water into the teapot.

'So was the wolf.'

'I mean I'm sorry I haven't seen him. Sit down then, tea's made.'

'No signs?' persisted Mrs Eckles, flopping down. 'He likes to leave a trail, let folks know he's been. No dead rats? Bits o' mice? Scattered feathers? Dismembered fox?'

'No.'

A little silence fell while Clover poured the tea. She opened the sugar pot, which contained a solitary lump, and popped it in Mrs Eckles' cup.

'I likes four,' grumbled Mrs Eckles. 'I gotta sweet tooth.'

'I know. Sorry. We're out.'

'I 'ad a portrait done of 'im once,' mused Mrs Eckles. 'A passin' picture-maker done it.' She raised her cup and took a noisy slurp.

'Where is it?'

''E didn't like it. Clawed it to shreds. Went for the picture-maker. Nearly 'ad 'is ear off. Probably because 'e came on a horse. Neville don't like horses, not since he got kicked by one. 'E'll be back today, I reckon.'

''Course he will,' said Clover, opening the oven door. 'He'll be missing his huge toy collection by now.'

'Them biscuits smells nice. Got raisins in, 'ave they?'

'Yes. I almost confused them with the mouse droppings. Anyway, I used the last of them. The flour's all gone, too. We're pretty well out of every-thing. I think one of us had better go to the village.'

'You,' said Mrs Eckles firmly. 'I gotta stay in for Neville.'

'All right,' said Clover. 'Will you make the list?'

'You do it. You know what's needed. Tell 'im to put it on the slate. Just make sure you get plenty o' sugar lumps. An' Neville's milk, he likes full cream. When you gets back, you can start sortin' out the loft, where you're sleepin'.'

'All right,' said Clover. She was looking forward to that. 'I'll do it as soon as I've finished down here.'

'Looks like it's all done,' said Mrs Eckles, staring around.

'Not quite. I haven't done the cupboard in the corner.'

The cupboard in the corner was the only one she hadn't tackled. It was a narrow floor-to-ceiling cupboard squeezed between the wall and the chimney breast in a dark, shadowy recess. The latch was secured with a sturdy padlock. There was no sign of the key.

'Oh, you don't need to bother with that,' said Mrs Eckles quickly.

'I don't?'

'No. That's me private cupboard. I keeps all me gear in there. Stuff for me remedies. Some of it's a bit – volatile. Needs careful handlin'. Ain't been in there meself fer a while. Lost the key. Keeps it on a string round me neck, but it musta dropped off. That's another thing gone missin'. You ain't come across it, I s'pose?'

'No. Sorry.'

'Oh well. Don't need it right now anyway. Not a lot o' witchin' work lately. Punters 'ave been stayin' away, dunno why.'

'Perhaps they're put off by the state of the front garden.' Clover shovelled the hot biscuits on to a plate. 'It's a bit unwelcoming. And that gate can be very rude.'

'It's *supposed* to be unwelcoming. I'm a witch, not the good fairy. Folks expect an air o' doom an' gloom.'

'No point if it puts them off coming, though, is there? You should cheer it up. Put in a tub of daffodils. I'll do it, when I've got time. How many biscuits do you want?'

'Four,' said Mrs Eckles. 'Mustn't be greedy.'

She was, though. She had seven.

The village was called Tingly Bottom. It lay on the edge of the forest and consisted of a sprinkling of cottages, a tavern and a tiny shop run by Mr and Mrs Trowzer. Mr Trowzer had a swollen, purple face and moved in excruciatingly slow motion. His wife sat in the back room, adding up columns of figures at snail-like speed. Together, they were known as the Pair Of Old Trowzers. Privately, Clover thought they could do with a bit of zip.

Three customers stood at the shop counter – Mrs Pluck, Mistress Vittles and the Widow McFinn. Mrs Pluck was talking to Mr Trowzer in a loud voice.

'. . . and if it was my girl,' she was saying, 'I'd have something to say about it. I don't care how good the money is, you don't send your own flesh an' blood out –'

She broke off with a guilty little gasp as the bell tinkled and Clover entered the shop. Mr Trowzer's puffy purple head wobbled slowly in her direction, like a tortoise scenting a dandelion.

'Morning,' said Clover. Mrs Pluck went pink and fumbled for her purse.

'Goo-morn-in-young-lad-y,' intoned Mr Trowzer, very slowly.

'Morning, Clover,' said Mistress Vittles. 'We just seen your pa.'

'Did you now?'

'Yes. Weaving his way home from The Axes. Been there best part of the morning, it looks like. I hear you've taken the cleanin' job at Mrs Eckles'.'

'Goodness,' said Clover. 'Word gets around, doesn't it?'

'I must say I'm surprised at your ma,' said the Widow McFinn.

'Oh, you are? And why might that be?'

'Well. I mean. Sending you there.'

'She didn't *send* me. I chose to go.'

'She means it's not safe, dear,' explained Mrs Pluck.

'I can take care of myself.'

'Ah, but *can* you?' asked Mistress Vittles darkly. 'There's a lot o' strange goings-on in that cottage, 'specially after dark.'

'That's right,' butted in Mrs Pluck excitedly. 'My Reggie says only last night he was coming through the woods and he heard her out wailing amongst the trees, rattling a box o' bones. Shoutin' for the devil, he said. *Devil,* she went. *Come to me, devil!* Blood-curdlin', it was.'

'She was shouting for *Neville*,' said Clover. 'That's her cat. And she was rattling his biscuit tin. Have you finished? I'm in rather a hurry.'

'Riiiight-a-way-young-lad-y-riiiight-a-way,' droned Mr Trowzer, rubbing his hands in a leisurely fashion. 'Got-yer-list? The-lad-ies-were-just-a-go-ing.'

Clover took out her list. All three women squinted over her shoulder, trying to see what was written on it, probably hoping for eye of newt or a nice snake fillet. They showed no signs of leaving. She slapped it on the counter and stood in front of it, so they couldn't see.

'So what's it like in there, dear?' asked Mistress Vittles, her beady little eyes snapping with curiosity. 'Magical charms an' talismans? Mysterious signs chalked on the floor? Stinkin' brews bubblin' away –'

'No,' said Clover. 'Nothing like that. But it really isn't any of your business, is it?'

'Well I never!' snapped Mistress Vittles.

'If you're going to be like that!' sniffed Mrs Pluck.

'We'll leave,' announced the Widow McFinn through tight lips.

All three picked up their baskets and stalked from the shop with their noses in the air.

Mr Trowzer moved a bloated finger down Clover's list.

'Sug-ar,' he intoned. 'Miiiilk-floour-pep-per-coorns-cheeeeeeese . . .'

'Will this take long?' asked Clover, trying not to fidget.

'Take-a-fair-while-young-lad-y. Lot-o'-items-'ere. Too-much-to-fit-in-yer-liddle-bas-ket. Tell-you-what-I'll-do. I'll-box-it-up-an'-send-the-boy-round-with-it-later. 'Ow's-that?'

'Fine. I'll take the milk now, though, and the sugar. She particularly wants those.'

'Miiiiiiillllk,' wheezed Mr Trowzer. 'That'll-be-coolin'-out-the-back. Wait-there-young-lad-y-I'll-be-riiiight-back.' And he crawled off. After what seemed like years, he crawled back to enquire whether that would be full cream. Clover told him it would be. He crawled off again. The sugar took even longer, because he counted it out, maddeningly slowly, lump by lump.

Some considerable time later, Clover stepped into the street. It was empty apart from a man leaning against a wall. He had a gold ring in his ear and was chewing on a straw. He removed it from his mouth and said, 'You the lass who's cleaning for old Mother Eckles?'

Clover stopped and rolled her eyes in exasperation. Did everybody know her business?

'Yes,' she said shortly. 'What of it?'

'Got a message. Tell her the cart's ready. I'll bring it round day after tomorrow. Hire's gone up to three pence, tell her.'

'That's it?'

'Aye.'

And the man turned his back and strolled off down the street. Clover watched him for a moment, then set off in the opposite direction towards the forest.

Chapter Seven

He's Back!

Mrs Eckles was waiting by the gate, face beaming and arms full of what looked like festering carpet.

'Neville!' squealed Mrs Eckles. 'I've got 'im! He's back!'

'Welcome *home*, Miss Clover! Allow *me*,' said the gate in a new, rich, oily voice. It swung open, the height of smooth efficiency. Clover walked through. It closed behind her with a smart little click.

'I'll 'ave to do somethin' about that gate,' said Mrs Eckles. 'I can't stand it.'

'Only being pleasant,' said the gate.

'Ah, shut it,' said Mrs Eckles.

'I *am* shut,' pointed out the gate.

'I mean shut up *talkin'*. Enough with the barrier backchat. You're just a gate with a spell on, so stop puttin' on airs. Just a silly old stopgap, ain't it, Neville? Not like *you*. You're Mummy's baby, you are. Mummy's naughty baby who's been out in the woods fightin' the foxes again!'

She bent down and covered the festering carpet with kisses. It thrashed around in her arms, revealing itself to have legs, a head and a tail. It then clawed its way up her arm and slumped over her shoulder, purring rather wheezily.

So this was Neville. He was massive, with matted black fur and malevolent yellow eyes. His face was flat, as though he'd been fired from a cannon into a brick wall. Half of his left ear was missing and he smelled as though he'd been swimming in a swamp.

Clover put out a hand to stroke him. Instantly, the purr turned into a warning growl and his lips curled back, exposing a row of yellow fangs.

'Wary of strangers,' explained Mrs Eckles. 'He'll

be all right when he knows you. Did you get his milk?'

'I did.'

'Hear that, Neville? Come on, then, let's go and find yer bowl.'

They began walking up the path.

'The rest of the stuff's being delivered,' said Clover. 'Oh, and I met a man who said to tell you the cart's ready. He's bringing it round the day after tomorrow. And it's gone up to three pence.'

'Oh my!' Mrs Eckles gave a startled little gasp. 'Never! Is it that time already?'

'What time?'

'The May Fayre at Palsworthy. Forgot to check the calendar. Three pence, you say? Daylight robbery. It were two last year.'

'You're going to the Fayre?'

'Oh, yes. I goes every year, does well there. Sells me remedies, does readin's. Puts out a proper sign. They got respect fer witches up Palsworthy way.'

'Can I come?' asked Clover hopefully. A trip to the Fayre would be an adventure. She had never been, but knew it was held in a big meadow outside the busy market town of Palsworthy, a day's ride away.

'No room in the cart, not with all me stuff. No,

you'll stay 'ere. Keep an eye on the cottage. I'm only gone three days. Leave Friday, back Sunday. You'll be all right, won't you? You're sensible. The protection spells'll keep you safe. You'll 'ave Neville for company. And Wilf'll pop round.'

'Who?'

'Young Wilf, the delivery boy. Works for old Trowzer. Red hair. Freckles.'

'Oh yes,' said Clover. 'I've seen him around. The one with scabby knees.'

'That's 'im. He stayed 'ere last time I went. But it weren't an ideal arrangement. 'E means well, but 'e's terrible clumsy.'

'I'll be fine,' said Clover. 'Although I don't know about Neville.'

'I'd take 'im with me, but he don't like it in the cart. Last time he wouldn't eat his food. Widdled in me slipper. Attacked a coupla punters an' all. Drew blood. Highly strung, ain't you, my angel? But it ain't good for business.'

'I'll bet,' said Clover, glancing at the angel who was giving her filthy looks from behind Mrs Eckles' neck.

They had reached the kitchen door. Mrs Eckles put Neville down and he twined lovingly around her ankles.

'He understands everything you say, you know,' said Mrs Eckles.

'Mm,' said Clover doubtfully. 'Well, I'll give him his milk and put the kettle on. I expect you'd like a cuppa?'

'Later,' said Mrs Eckles, with a small sigh. 'First I gotta go out pickin'.'

'What, now? In broad daylight? I thought witches always picked at midnight, under a full moon.'

'Not likely. I've 'ad enough o' the forest at night for the time bein'. Flippin' chilly out there. No, I'd best go now. Run outa herbs an' whatnot. Need to make up fresh remedies, now the Fayre's comin' up. Want to get most of it done tonight, so I can rest up tomorrer. Put me feet up. Spend some quality time with Neville.'

'All right,' said Clover. 'While you're gone, I'll make a start on my room.'

'Aye. Listen out fer Wilf. I'll leave a penny tip on the table. Give 'im a bit o' cake.'

'I thought we'd finished the cake.'

'That were the last one. Another one arrived this mornin', when I was out lookin' fer Mr Naughty. I've stuck it in the pantry.'

'Get them delivered, do you?'

'Nope. Somebody leaves 'em on the doorstep.

Grateful punter, I reckon.'

'That's nice,' said Clover. 'Shows you're appreciated.'

'It do, don't it? I've 'ad four so far. Ginger, cherry, fruit, an' this one's chocolate. 'Course, I ran a routine safety spell over the first one, just to make sure it weren't poisoned. Can't be too careful. Nothin' amiss, so I ate it. Lovely, it was.'

'Oh well,' said Clover. 'You've got a secret admirer. Nothing wrong with that.'

'Nope.' Mrs Eckles reached for an old wicker basket behind the kitchen door. 'Right, I'm off. When Wilf comes in, remind him to duck under the low beam.'

'All right.'

'Don't let nobody else in, mind.'

'All right.'

'I'm very particular who comes in me cottage. There's some funny types around. Types who might try an' *trick* their way in. Pretend to be what they ain't. Offer you stuff free.'

'Like cake?'

'No, no, I've already said cake's all right. Any more o' those arrive, bring 'em in. But nothin' else unless I gives you the say-so. Especially tomatoes, or any other form of fruit.'

'I'm not about to accept any poisoned apples from old peddler women, if that's what you mean. I'm not daft.'

'No,' said Mrs Eckles. 'I know you ain't. Just remember to watch out, is all. I'll be back before sundown.'

'Right. I'll make us some dumplings for supper.'

'Dumplin's, eh?' Mrs Eckles sounded pleased. 'Bin a while since I 'ad them. Keep an eye out fer that missin' key. I'll be needin' to get in that cupboard now.'

Clover stood next to the trapdoor, looking around at her very own bedroom. It was under the eaves at the very top of the house. You reached it by climbing a short ladder outside Mrs Eckles' bedroom, which was firmly locked. Clover had no idea what it was like in there. Judging by the state of the kitchen, she wasn't sure she wanted to know.

It was a tiny space and you had to keep your head down to avoid braining yourself on the beams. There was nothing in there except cobwebs, a low rickety table, an empty chest of drawers and a narrow bed with a straw mattress. It was dark, too. The tiny window was black with grime and hardly let in any light. But she would soon fix that.

For the next hour she raced up and down, arms full of thin sheets, old blankets and pails of soapy water. She chased away spiders and bats. She made up the bed, neatly placing her nightie under the pillow. After a fight, she managed to get the window open. It looked out over the back garden. The cherry tree was directly opposite. The tip of one of its branches extended almost to the ivy-clad window sill. If she leaned out, she could nearly touch it.

Under the kitchen sink she found a chipped china jug and wash bowl, which she carried up and placed on the table, together with her washing things. She found a candle and a box of matches, which also went on the table. She got out her sewing box and made a simple curtain for the window, using a length of string and a square piece of old cloth, which she took the trouble to hem. She found a hammer and a box of nails, two of which she hammered into a beam, so that she could hang up her cloak and blue dress. The rest of her worldly possessions – the ribbons, the stockings and the drawers – she placed neatly in the chest.

She was out gathering honeysuckle in the back garden when she heard muffled voices, one of them unmistakably oily, followed by the sound of the gate clanging shut. There was the sound of approaching footsteps and a boy came staggering around the side of the cottage, carrying a large box piled high with a lot of slippery little packages wrapped in greased paper.

The boy had a freckled face topped with a shock of flaming red hair. He had big ears, too. The sun shone through them. What with that and the hair, it looked like someone had set fire to his head.

'I've got to put this down,' said the boy rather desperately.

'Hello,' said Clover. 'You must be Wilf.'

'Yep,' said Wilf. 'That's me.'

He hoisted the box to get a better grip. A paper bag full of coffee beans slithered sideways and fell to the grass, bursting open and scattering beans everywhere. Flo and Doris, the chickens, came strutting up, hoping for extra breakfast.

'Oops!' said Wilf. 'Sorry. Look, I've *really* got to put this down. Mrs Eckles in?' He was trying to balance the box and scrape up the beans with his foot. Flo pecked him on the ankle. '*Ow*. Get off, Flo.'

'No. She left a tip, though. Said to give you some cake.'

'There's cake?'

'Yes.'

'With sugar icing? And a cherry in the middle?'

'No. Why?'

'I dunno. No reason.' Wilf looked a bit puzzled, then shook his head. 'I really don't know why I said that. Ow, get *off*, you two!' Doris was now joining in the attack on his ankle.

'Well, this one's chocolate. Look, just leave the beans, I'll pick them up later. Wipe your feet, please, I've done the floor.'

Clover led the way in, with Wilf trudging behind her. She couldn't help feeling pleased when she heard his gasp of surprise.

'Wow! What's been happening here?' He was hovering in the doorway, mouth open.

'Tidied up a bit, that's all,' said Clover rather smugly. 'I'm Clover Twig, by the way. Mrs Eckles hired me to clean. Put the box on the table. I'll get the –'

There was a sudden cry, and she turned just in time to see Wilf trip over the mat and crash heavily on to his knees. The box of groceries shot from his arms, overturning the rocking chair. A bag of flour burst open in a white explosion. A small round cheese went careering off into a corner.

A cabbage rolled across the floor, ending up at the cat basket, where Neville was currently sleeping. He opened one eye, registered Wilf's presence, sighed and firmly closed it again. Clover had the feeling he had seen it all before.

'Oops. Sorry about that.'

Wilf straightened, cracked his head on the low beam, staggered back into a bucket of soapy water and fell over again, backwards this time.

Clover felt a bit guilty. She had forgotten to remind him about the beam. Mrs Eckles was right. He was certainly accident-prone.

Chapter Eight

Let's Have a Look!

'Are you all right?' Clover asked. Wilf was sitting in a puddle of water, looking groggy and not sure which bit of himself to rub first. 'Look – just sit down before anything else happens. I mean, stand up, then sit down properly.'

'Sorry about that,' said Wilf, climbing to his feet. 'I'll clear it all up. Just as soon as the twinkling little stars have gone away.'

He collapsed on to a chair, clutching his head.

Clover noticed that his knuckles were red and skinned. His ragged shorts had holes in. His knees were covered in scabs and bruises.

Clover took the chocolate cake from the pantry, a knife from the orderly knife drawer and a clean plate from the clean plate cupboard. She cut a large slice and placed it before him.

'Here,' she said.

Neville opened one yellow eye, then the other. He stood up, gave a leisurely stretch, padded across and thumped heavily on to Wilf's lap.

'Hello there, Nev,' said Wilf, tugging his good ear. 'You got home all right, then.'

Neville drooled and kneaded his claws, eyes fixed hopefully on the cake.

Clover began to restore order. She pulled the rocking chair upright, set the box the right way up and recovered the cheese and the cabbage. Behind her, Wilf was greedily chomping into the cake, pausing only to offer Neville little licks of chocolate from his fingers.

'You shouldn't do that,' scolded Clover. 'It's unhygienic. He's spoiled enough as it is.'

'I dunno,' said Wilf easily. 'It's a bad thing if you can't be spoiled a bit when you're over a hundred years old. Isn't that right, Nev?'

'A *hundred*? I don't think cats live that long.'

'Witch cats do, Mrs Eckles says. She reckons he understands everything you say.'

'All cat owners say that,' said Clover. 'I don't believe it, though.'

'He belonged to her grandma, did she tell you? Passed down, along with the cottage. Everything else went to her sister.'

'The one she rowed with over the cherry tree?' Clover reached for the mop.

'That's the one. Bit of a family feud. I hope you're a good listener, she loves a good old moan.'

'Do you know her well, then?'

'Not really. I just pop in now and then. Me and Grampy are her nearest neighbours. Nobody comes here much. I think they find the place a bit off-putting. Especially from the front. The windows stare, did you notice?'

'They don't bother me. I just stare back.'

'The gate doesn't help either. One day rude, the next day over-friendly.'

'You're right there,' agreed Clover. 'Far too much to say for itself.'

'You're not scared, then? Staying here?'

'No. Should I be?'

'Well, you know.'

'What? What do I know?'

'You know. The rumours.'

'What rumours?'

'Ah, nothing.'

'No, go on. What rumours?'

'No, really, I don't want to –'

'*What rumours?*'

'Well, they do say the cottage disappears from time to time.'

'Well, yes,' said Clover. 'On a foggy day, I dare say it does. Lift your feet up, I'm trying to mop.'

'I'm just telling you what they say. You don't have to believe it. Though Grampy tells a funny story. About when he was a small boy. Mrs Eckles was old even then, he says.'

'How old is your grampy?'

'I don't know. Ninety?'

'Then how is that possible? That'd make her at least a hundred and forty.'

'Don't ask me. Do you want to hear this or don't you?'

'All right,' said Clover. 'I can't wait. Go on.'

'Grampy's about six or seven, and he wakes in the night, and he's hungry. Nothing in the pantry to eat. So he climbs out of the window and comes here to pinch a handful of cherries from her tree. And guess what?'

'The fog comes down and the cottage disappears?' said Clover sceptically.

'No fog. It was a clear night. But the cottage has disappeared all right. Just a huge hole in the ground where it should have been. The garden's all of a tip and all. The log pile had collapsed, he said, and there were loads of creepers torn up by the roots. The privy lying on its side. But mostly, that huge hole. Gave him a terrible shock.'

'So what did he do?'

'Ran home and stuck his head under the pillow. Didn't say anything because he wasn't supposed to be out stealing cherries from a witch's garden in the middle of the night. A day or two later, he plucks up the courage to come by to have a look, and everything's back to normal.'

'He probably dreamed it,' said Clover. 'Sounds like a dream to me.'

'That's what I said. But he just tells me to shut up, he knows what he saw. And that's the story. Any more of that cake?'

'Loads. I'll wrap up a piece, you can take it with you.'

'Trying to get rid of me?'

'Well, I am a bit busy.'

Clover cut another slice and went to the drawer for paper to wrap it in. Wilf's eye fell on the sugar pot. He reached in, took a lump and awkwardly tossed it into the air, opening his mouth to catch it.

It hit him hard in the eye, bounced off, and fell on the floor.

'Ah, *heck*!' he said, rubbing his eye. 'How come I can never do that?'

'Why would you want to?'

'I dunno. I just do. I've tried for years and never done it once. I even dream about doing it. Most nights, actually.'

'Well, it's a very silly dream. Daft dreams must run in your family. Here's your cake.'

Clover handed him the neatly wrapped slice and pointedly picked up the bucket.

'All right, I can take a hint,' said Wilf. 'Got another delivery to do anyway.'

He stood up. In doing so, he knocked the cake on to the floor with his elbow. The plate broke in half and the cake landed upside down in an unpleasant brown splodge. It seemed he couldn't move without destroying something.

'Oops! Sorry about that. I'll try gluing the

plate . . . '

'No, no,' said Clover, exasperated now. 'Just leave it.'

'Then I'll help scrape up the –'

'No. Really. Just go. Don't forget your tip.'

She nodded at the penny on the table. Wilf scooped it up and rummaged around in his pockets for a bit, looking for something.

'Ah,' he said at last. 'Here it is. Found it in the grass just outside the gate. I think it belongs to Mrs Eckles.'

It was a padlock key.

'I reckon so,' said Clover. 'She said she was missing a key. Thanks.'

She reached out a hand. Wilf made no move to pass it over. He just stood looking at it in his palm.

'It's the one to the corner cupboard, right?' he said.

'Right.'

'Thought so. Ever seen in there?'

'No.'

'Nor me. She's very secretive about it. Shall we have a look?'

'What?'

'While she's gone. Let's have a look.'

'Certainly not!' Clover was scandalised. 'Whatever are you thinking?'

'I'm thinking I'd like a look in that cupboard. I bet there's all kinds of stuff.'

'Well, I must say I'm shocked. She thinks you're a trustworthy sort of boy.'

'I am. But I'm still curious. Come on. Just a quick peek. We won't touch anything.'

'No,' said Clover firmly. She reached out and took the key from his palm. 'I'm in charge while she's out and you're not going anywhere near that cupboard. Shouldn't you be getting on?'

'I suppose so. You're sure I can't help?'

'No. Just go.'

'Ta for the cake.'

'You're welcome. Goodbye.'

''Bye then.'

On the way out, Wilf banged his head on the doorway.

'*Ow!*'

Then he tripped over the step.

'*Ouch!*'

Clover waited while his footsteps crunched around the side of the house and down the path. Would he?

'*Aaargh!*'

'Oh, sir! Sir! How *did* you manage to *do* that, sir . . .'

Yes. He had trapped his fingers in the gate.

Clover shut the door firmly.

Chapter Nine

Though I Say it Myself, I'm Good

Time for a second visit to Castle Coldiron, where events are continuing apace.

This time, we are in a boudoir – a room full of purple drapes, scarlet cushions and scattered shoes. Mesmeranza, clad in a green velvet robe, is seated at her dressing table in front of a large mirror with an ornate gilt frame. The mirror is very flattering. It gives out a candlelit glow, irons out wrinkles, reduces noses, and generally doesn't so much reflect as improve.

Miss Fly is perched on a hard chair by the door, in a draught. It is late afternoon and she has been up since dawn, woken by a posse of cats demanding breakfast, closely followed by a large chunk of her bedroom ceiling falling down.

Let's listen in.

'So,' said Miss Fly, dabbing her poor sore nose, which if anything is even redder. She can no longer pronounce her t's or her m's. 'Did id go well last nide? With the boy?'

'It went very well, Fly,' said Mesmeranza. 'Though I say it myself, I'm good.' She picked up a lipstick, leaned closer to the mirror and began to paint her lips.

'*Perfect,*' murmured the flattering mirror. The honey-eyed tones oozed from somewhere deep within the glass. 'Red is soooo *good* on you. If I may suggest, perhaps a *touch* more rouge?'

'Did you find oud everything you – *achoo!* – need do know?' enquired Miss Fly.

'Not *quite* everything. He couldn't tell me anything about the girl. But I was right about one thing. He adores cake. I told you, didn't I? Root vegetables indeed! I don't know why I bother listening to you, I'm always right. Tell Mrs Chunk this one must be simply *irresistible*. White sugar icing with a cherry on top. Write it down.'

Miss Fly took out her little black book and noted it down.

'He didund recognise you, then?'

'Of *course* not! How could he? I am the mistress of disguise, you know that. Anyway, I wiped his memory with the Hypnospecs. I must say they worked brilliantly well. Grandmother's inventions were built to last. She was a very good witch, you know.'

'Don'd you bean bad?'

'Don't tell me what I mean. I mean she was good at being bad. Bad, devious and clever. Like me.'

Mesmeranza inspected her reflection and patted her smooth hair.

'Ooh, *yes*,' whispered the mirror. 'That's it . . . the *hair* now, the beautiful *hair* . . .'

'So the boy's looking after the coddage again this year? You found that oud?'

'Actually, he didn't seem too sure.'

'So you *didund* find out whad you wanded do know, then.'

Crash! Miss Fly jumped as Mesmeranza slammed down her hairbrush.

'Typical! This is *so* typical of you, Fly! Casting doubts, picking holes! Just stop your wittering and concentrate on your own side of things. Did you find the Umbrella? And the Wand?'

'Nod yed,' confessed Miss Fly. 'Id really is a derrible dip up there. Id's all dark, I can'd see a thing. You should ged a ban with a card in do sord id oud.'

'A *what*?'

'A *ban*. With a *card*.'

'Oh, a *man* with a *cart*! Do speak properly, it's like having a conversation with a drain.'

'Bud I'b jusd saying. All those old boxes and chests. They're baking the floor sag. If you god in a ban with a card –'

'*Stop telling me what to do!* The Plan, Fly! That's what I must concentrate on. I can't get a *man* in *now*. The Fayre's in two days' time and that's when I pounce.'

'Bud the castle's cubbing down around our ears! By bedroob's under the attic and the ceiling's falling down in chunks . . .'

'Don't bother me with trivia! I let you live here rent free, lovely apartment, fabulous views. I even let you keep your wretched cat posse, getting their filthy hairs everywhere. And in return I require some light secretarial duties. Is that too much to ask?'

Mesmeranza snatched up a silver compact and

began furiously powdering her nose.

'That's it,' murmured the mirror soothingly. 'A little touch of powder . . . *ooh . . . gorgeous . . .*'

'I suppose nod,' sighed Miss Fly. Her nose dripped on to her little black book.

'I should think not. I take it you haven't found the Poncho?'

'No.'

'So it's hey-ho up to the attic again then, isn't it? I suggest you go and put your oldest, horridest clothes on. Oh, wait a minute! I've just noticed, you're wearing them already. By the way, I take it you mentioned the dungeon inspection to Chunk?'

'No,' said Miss Fly. Nervously, her hand went to her cardigan pocket. Down there, amongst all the screwed-up hankies, was yet another note. It had been slipped under her door at some point during the night.

'Well, don't forget. Tell him I shall be down later today.'

'Very well,' said Miss Fly, sounding like she wanted to weep.

'And do stop sounding so *moany*. I do believe your continual carping is giving me *wrinkles*. See? There's a new one, right *here*. *Your* fault.'

Crossly, Mesmeranza leaned towards the mirror.

Carefully, she lifted her hand and placed a red, sharp-ended finger over the small furrow between her eyebrows.

'Hold still . . .' purred the mirror. 'Won't take a moment . . .'

Mesmeranza kept still, with her finger on the crease. She kept it there for a long moment, staring hard at her reflection.

'There,' whispered the mirror. 'All done.'

Mesmeranza took the finger away. The furrow had vanished. Her brow was perfectly smooth.

That's Magic Mirrors for you.

Chapter Ten

A Cosy Place to Be

'Dumplin's,' said Mrs Eckles, speaking indistinctly because her mouth was full of them. 'I loves 'em, I do. Know what my grandmother said once? You can beat an egg, but you can't beat a dumplin'. 'Ow we laughed. Well, we 'ad to make the most of 'er jokes, she didn't make 'em often.'

They were sitting at the kitchen table, eating supper. The curtains were drawn, a fire burned merrily in the hearth and the lamps were lit. The kettle sang on the hob. Outside, in the forest, night was falling and the owls were out. Neville was in his basket, sides heaving and claws flexing as he hunted down dream mice. The kitchen was a cosy place to be.

'What was she like?' asked Clover. 'Was she strict?'

'Who, Grandmother? Oooh, a terrible tarter. Not much of a child lover. Spent most of 'er time workin' on 'er inventions behind closed doors. You wouldn't want to cross her, 'specially when she'd been messin' about with 'er poisons. She didn't always wash her 'ands. We 'ad to be careful at tea-time.'

'She'd poison her own *grandchildren*?'

'Oh, not badly. Just enough to give us bellyache. We was s'posed to spot it. You never knew where she put it, could be in the parsnips or the trifle. We always ran a safety spell, to be on the safe side. If it glowed orange, you didn't ask fer second 'elpin's.' Mrs Eckles chuckled and stared at Clover. 'Don't look so shocked. It were all part o' the trainin'. She said you never know who's out to get yer, and she was right.'

'But she was your *grandmother*!'

'Sometimes relatives is the worst. And she was a witch. It's all fair game to a witch. They experiments on anybody around.'

'They do?' Clover quickly put down her fork.

Mrs Eckles gave another little chuckle and speared another dumpling.

'Well, some of 'em do. Ah, don't worry, I ain't like that. You'll notice *I* always washes me 'ands when I been out pickin'.'

'Did you get everything you wanted?' asked Clover, nodding at the battered old basket by the door. It was filled to the brim with toadstools and bunches of strange herbs she didn't recognise.

'Pretty much. Nice patch o' Funglewart by the stream, I was lucky to spot it. Couldn't find any Slipweasel, but I'm hopin' there's some left in the cupboard. If it ain't slipped out through a crack. Sneaky stuff, Slipweasel.'

'Oh – talking of that, I think this might be the key,' said Clover, suddenly remembering and taking it from her apron pocket.

'It is!' cried Mrs Eckles, snatching it. 'Clever girl! Where'd you find it?'

'I didn't. Wilf did. It was by the gate, he said.'

'Well, there's an omen. It's been a day o' good luck fer me. Neville, the Funglewart and now the key. Three things. Bodes well for the Fayre. Reckon I'll rake it in this year. Need to an' all. Lot o' repairs need doin' to the cottage.'

Mrs Eckles tucked the key into her pocket, speared yet another dumpling and set to with renewed energy.

'Mrs Eckles?' said Clover. 'Can I ask you something?'

'Mmm?'

'If you're a witch, why don't you just *magic* yourself some money? Or say a – I don't know – thatch-repairing spell? Or something?'

Mrs Eckles appeared to give this some thought. She set down her fork and sat chewing. Then she said, '"Twouldn't be right. That'd just be benefitin' meself, see. That's not what it's all about. A witch is there for others. Although there's Someone I Could Mention who don't see it that way.'

'So magic's not an option,' said Clover.

'Oh, it's an *option*. I *could* do it. But I prefers not to. You shouldn't waste yer energies on run-o'-the-mill stuff. That'd be Misuse O' Power. One o' the first rules in the book. 'Course there's Someone I Could Mention who skips that chapter.'

She gave Clover a hopeful little glance. It was very clear that she was dying to tell who the Someone was.

'Like who?' asked Clover.

'Mesmeranza,' said Mrs Eckles through tight lips.

'My rotten sister. She's never stuck with the rules, that one.'

At that point, Neville's yellow eyes snapped open and he made an odd noise that was a sort of cross between a growl and a whimper. His fur stood up first – then the rest of him. He arose from his basket and slunk across to the door, where he sat, pointedly glaring.

'He wants to go out,' said Mrs Eckles. 'Let him.'

Clover opened the door. Outside, there was a cold wind blowing up. It sneaked through the door, causing the candles to flicker. Neville vanished into the dark. Clover stood there for a moment, peering into the shadows. Nobody there, but for some reason, she had the uncomfortable feeling that she was being watched. Hastily, she retreated inside and shot the bolts across.

'He don't like Mez,' said Mrs Eckles. 'One mention of 'er name an' 'e's off. Cats always know who don't like 'em. Well, they do when they're on the end of a boot.'

'She's not a cat lover, then?'

'Nah. The times I 'ad to rescue 'im from down the well. When we was kids, she was always danglin' 'im over ravines by 'is tail, just to taunt me. We're opposites, we are. Never got on. Ain't spoken fer years.

Not since the business with the cottage.'

'What business would that be?'

'Well, Grandmother left it to me, see. She knew it was all I wanted. That an' Neville. Never 'ad much ambition, me. Not like Mez. She wants it all. Well, not Neville, she don't want him. But everything else. She's that jealous. Can't bear the thought o' me livin' 'ere. Even though she got the castle.'

'Castle? What castle?'

'Castle Coldiron. When we was growin' up, we lived there with Grandmother. Away in the mountains. Chilly bloomin' place. You didn't think we lived 'ere, did you? Grandmother weren't the type to live in a cottage. It weren't her style. She 'ardly ever used it. Me and Mez did, though. Spent hours muckin' about in it. Days, sometimes. She didn't care. Kept us out of her hair.'

'What – you mean you lived here in the forest all alone? She built it for you, as a – sort of playhouse?'

'Oh no. She didn't build it. This place is *old*, Clover. Been in the family for generations. Anyway, it kept us amused. When Grandmother was busy inventin' things, we 'ardly ever saw 'er. 'Cept at mealtimes. Very particular about us havin' three square meals a day. Got in terrible trouble if we wasn't punctual.'

'But if the cottage is here and the castle's far away in the mountains, how did you get back three times a d— oh, wait a minute. You're witches. You used broomsticks, I suppose.'

'Somethin' like that. You're learnin'. Yes, we spent a lot o' time 'ere in the cottage. But Coldiron was our 'ome. Mez got everything in it. The furnishin's an' fittin's, the staff, everythin'. All Grandmother's old stuff. 'Er magical inventions and whatnot.'

'Like what?' asked Clover, interested.

'Well now, let me see.' Mrs Eckles began ticking things off on her fingers. 'The Wand. The Mirror of Eternal Youth. The Poncho of Imperceptibility. The Hat of Shadows, the Hypnospecs, the Bad Weather Umbrella, the Crystal Ball, the Cabinet of Poisons. Booboo, o' course. Oh, and the Seven League Boots which she chucked out. Said she wouldn't be seen dead in 'em. Wrong sorta heels.' Mrs Eckles gave a disgusted little sniff.

'Sounds like she got a lot more than her fair share,' said Clover.

'She did. But I don't care. Not a great one for gadgets, me. Mirrors, Crystals, Hypnospecs, all that malarkey. You can keep it. Don't even bother with the broom much these days, too bloomin' draughty. A few basic skills, a clear brain, a cat and a cottage, that's all a witch needs if she's any good. The rest is all show.'

'What's that word you said? Hippo something?'

'Hypnospecs. Glasses what you stick on when you needs to put someone under the influence. Never look directly into a pair of Hypnospecs, Clover. Trick is to look away before the little green lights start whizzin'.'

'I'll remember that. Um – Poncho of whatever that word you said?'

'Imperceptibility. Makes you invisible. Scratchy bloomin' thing. Not one of Grandmother's better efforts. Funny to watch 'er knittin' it, though. Clickin' away with empty needles, feelin' the air to see 'ow long it was getting.'

'Hat of Shadows?'

'Wear it and no one can see yer face properly. Good for disguises.'

'Bad Weather Umbrella?'

'You puts it up fer bad weather.'

'Just an ordinary umbrella, then.'

'Nah. With an ordinary umbrella, you *waits* for bad weather to happen. A Bad Weather Umbrella *causes* it. Grandmother's 'ad a pattern on, as I recall. Little lightnin' bolts.'

'I see,' said Clover thoughtfully. She stood and

began collecting up the dishes. 'Um – Booboo?'

'The 'orse. Mez is welcome to 'im, 'e's a moody blighter. Nips, given half a chance. Got to watch 'im when 'e's standin' behind you wearin' his special Vanishin' Saddle. Another one o' Grandmother's brainwaves. Makes 'im invisible. Can't see 'is teeth comin'. Fair turn o' speed, though, 'specially in the air.'

'Air?' said Clover, startled.

''Course, you gotta watch he don't smack you round the 'ead with a wing.'

'*Wing?*'

''E can fly, didn't I say? I 'ave to admit 'e's good at findin' his own way 'ome, like pigeons. You could call 'im an 'omin' 'orse. Always best to send 'im 'ome once you've arrived where you're goin'. Wouldn't want 'im standin' around be'ind you, that's fer sure. Ain't my idea of a pet. Not a patch on my Neville.'

'Of course he's not,' said Clover. She meant it too. Neville smelled bad and had some horrible habits, but she would choose him any time over an invisible flying horse that nipped. Even if it did find its own way home.

'I loves my Nev, I do,' said Mrs Eckles fondly. 'What I likes about 'im is his intelligence. He takes it all in, you know. Everything you say.'

'What's the Mirror of Eternal Youth?' asked Clover, pouring hot water into the sink.

'Look in it every morning and it stops yer face crumblin'. Keeps Mez lookin' young enough to be me granddaughter. 'Ow she rubs *that* in.'

'I thought you never spoke?'

'She sent me a picture once with a note sayin' *Bet you wish you looked like this*. Know what I did? To get me own back? I sent 'er a picture o' the cottage an' wrote MINE in big black letters.' Mrs Eckles guffawed loudly, then added, 'What you lookin' at me funny for? It's all true. I ain't a batty old woman makin' all this up.'

'I'm sure you're not,' said Clover, sprinkling soap flakes. 'But I was just thinking. If your sister's got a whole castle to herself, why would she care about an old cottage? I mean, I know it's – er – cosy. But it hardly seems . . .'

'It's special,' said Mrs Eckles. 'Oh yes. Don't look much, but it's very special, this cottage.'

'Memories of happy times?' Clover stifled a little yawn as she frothed up the washing-up water. Fascinating though Mrs Eckles' ramblings were, it had been a long day. Tiredness was coming over her in waves.

'Dunno about *'appy*,' said Mrs Eckles. 'I'd say . . .

interestin'. Days in this cottage could just fly by.'

'Oh well,' said Clover. 'You got what you wanted. It's yours.'

'Mmm. Mez still ain't given up tryin' to get 'er 'ands on it, mind. Sometimes when I'm out in the garden I can feel 'er watchin' through the Crystal. Waitin' for me to let me guard down. Go off somewhere an' forget to renew the protection spells. She's probably watchin' now.'

'Really?' Clover glanced at the door.

'Ah, don't worry, you're safe. She can't see *inside*. And she can't come in either, unless she's invited over the threshold.' Mrs Eckles reached forward and threw another log on the fire. 'Tell you what, girl, why don't you leave that 'til the mornin'? Looks like you could do with a bit o' shut-eye. Besides, I got a long night ahead. Only room fer one of us workin'.'

'But I haven't washed up.'

'I'll wash up.'

'Ah, but you won't, will you?'

'I will. I *will*. But I makes a mess when I'm workin'. I can't have you standin' around fussin' an' tuttin' an' tryin' to clear up after me. You go on up. And don't worry if you hear noises in the night. I gotta brush up the protection spells, and that involves chantin'. I'll try and keep it down.'

'Right.'

'Ignore any funny smells. It gets a bit whiffy.'

'Right.'

'Whatever you hear, don't pay no mind. Just me, workin'.'

Chapter Eleven

Sleep Won't Come

Clover stood in her tiny loft bedroom. Oh, the luxury of having it all to herself. To find it just as she had left it – all clean and tidy. Nobody had hidden her nightdress. Nobody had used her comb and left it full of tangled hair. Nobody was fighting over the pillow.

Tired though she was, she went through the nightly ritual. Lit the candle. Combed out her hair, then plaited it again. Poured out cold, clean water and washed her face. Cleaned her teeth. Put on her nightie and hung her dress on the nail. And hurried across to the window.

Outside, there was a full moon and the sky was splashed with stars. The tips of the distant trees made a dark silhouette, like faraway mountains. Closer, she could hear the branches of the cherry tree rustling. From somewhere not so far away came a small, high-pitched screech, then silence. She hoped Neville had nothing to do with it.

Leaving the window ajar, because fresh air is good for you, she drew the curtain, hurried shivering across the bare boards and dived into the narrow bed. She blew out the candle, snuggled down, closed her eyes . . .

And failed to sleep.

She lay on her back. She lay on her side. Then her other side. Then her tummy. Then her back again. She tried counting sheep, but got bored after twenty. She sat up, thumped her pillow and lay down again. She tried counting ducks going to market, frogs leaping over lily pads and geese flying south for the winter. None of them worked.

The trouble was, the bed was strange. The mattress didn't mould itself to the shape of her body like the one at home. There was no one breathing beside her. No one rolling over and taking all the blanket. No one throwing out a sleepy arm and whacking her in the eye. No Little Herby appearing ghost-like around the curtain, whimpering because he'd had a scary dream.

There were strange noises too. Creaks and groans as the timbers cooled and the old cottage settled down for the night. Little scuttlings in the wainscot as the mice went about their business. Little tappings as the ivy brushed against the window pane. Swishing noises from the cherry tree. Her own cottage made noises at night as well – all old buildings do – but these were unfamiliar.

She thought about home. Pa's snores would be rattling the rafters. Ma would be mumbling, 'Stop *doin'* that, you three,' in her sleep. Her sisters would be dead to the world, arms flung out in a tangle of bedclothes. Herby would be lying in his little cot, thumb stuck in his mouth and small hands twitching.

She missed them. Quite a lot, actually.

Suddenly, there was a scrabbling noise from the window. Seconds later, a huge weight landed on her middle, driving all the air from her lungs. It felt like a ton of bricks – except that bricks don't smell like old carpet.

It was Neville. His huge, flat face loomed before

her. His whiskers tickled her chin. His paws were kneading the blanket, and he was purring and dribbling, clearly back from fox patrol and ready to settle down for the night.

'Get *off*, Neville,' Clover said, struggling to sit up. Neville hooked his claws into the pillow, determined to stay right where he was.

'You can't sleep here,' she scolded. 'You're too big and stinky.'

She reached out in the darkness and fumbled for the matches. After a moment, she got the candle alight. On the bed, Neville was making himself at home. His yellow eyes blinked up at her happily. Firmly, she prised his claws loose, then wrapped her arms around his warm body.

'Miaaaaaaoooow,' he protested as she swung her legs on to the floor and stood up, heaving him with her.

'Come on. I'm taking you back downstairs.'

Arms full of cat, Clover pattered across the floor to the trapdoor. Neville scrambled up on to her shoulder and draped himself around her neck, like a fur scarf.

She lifted the trapdoor, carefully descended the ladder and walked along the short, dark landing to the flight of twisty stairs leading to the kitchen.

She was just about to go down, when she heard something.

A raised voice was coming from below. It belonged to Mrs Eckles. It sounded irate.

Clover crept down the stairs and poked her head around the corner.

The kitchen door was closed. But, being an old door, it didn't fit the frame properly. There was a gap beneath, and a thin strip of space at the top and sides. And through that gap and space poured light. Strange, acid green light that certainly wasn't made by an oil lamp or candle. It drifted lazily in the air, coiling like smoke and glowing before slowly fading to nothing.

Clover could make out words now. Angry words.

Mrs Eckles said, 'I'm tellin' you you're to *refuse*! That's my last word on the subject.'

'And I'm telling *you* I don't have a choice in the matter. It's the *rule*. It's written in the *manual*. There's no point in discussing it.'

The strange voice was high and squeaky, like it should belong to somebody – really *little*. Somebody with tiny little lungs and a miniature throat. Probably about the size of – what? A mouse? A mushroom? A – *fairy*? If it was a fairy, it was a very cross one.

'To blazes with the rule!' roared Mrs Eckles. '*You*

know what she's capable of. I don't put nothin' past 'er. She won't try anything while I'm here, but when my back's turned, that's a different matter. Whose side are you on, anyway?'

'It's not a question of taking sides. If I'm summoned, I have to obey orders. *You* know that. The manual clearly states –'

'Forget the blasted manual! I'm sick of hearin' you quote the manual at me! Treated you fair, ain't I? You ain't exactly 'ad to kill yerself with work.'

'So? It is a *part-time* job, you know.'

'*No* time more like!'

'Anyway,' went on the strange voice sulkily, 'anyway, it won't come to that. She can't get in, can she? Not if you've got the protection spells in place.'

'Course they're in place. What d'you take me for?'

'There you are, then. And you say you've got a reliable girl in this time. So what's all the fuss about?'

'I've got to cover all eventualities. Spells can be broken. Girls can be – *persuaded*. Sometimes, not very nicely. Do you want that on yer conscience?'

'Not my concern. I'm not breaking the rule.'

'I'm gonna open the door,' said Mrs Eckles disgustedly. 'I don't like the smell in 'ere.'

Her footsteps approached the door.

Quickly, Clover lifted Neville from behind her

neck, set him down and gave him a little nudge with her bare foot.

'Go on,' she whispered. 'You're on your own.'

And with that, she turned and fled back up the stairs, along the landing, up the ladder and into her bedroom. She lowered the trapdoor and shot the bolt across.

Shivering, she jumped into bed, blew out the candle, lay down and pulled the covers up over her ears.

It took her a long time to get to sleep.

Chapter Twelve

The Dungeon Inspection

Here we are again, back in Castle Coldiron. The weather has not improved. Storms are blowing in from the north. Miss Fly's cats are restless. They just slump around shedding hair, watching the clouds boil up and demanding more fish heads. Miss Fly is beside herself. Not only is her room filled with chunks of fallen ceiling plaster, but frankly, it's getting pongy.

Humperdump Chunk doesn't care about the worsening weather. He lives deep in the dark, dripping dungeons, where it's always the same. Hot, cold, day, night, war, peace – it's always the same in the dungeons.

Right now, he is in the guardroom. This is a fair-sized room with stone walls, dimly lit by a couple of oil lamps suspended crookedly from hooks. His head is sunk in his hands and his meaty elbows are propped on a small table, which contains an empty tin plate and a mug the size of a Yorkshire Terrier. It has a specially designed handle to accommodate his banana fingers.

The chair he is sitting on is heavily reinforced. It has to be, because Humperdump Chunk is BIG. Not only does he go a long way up, there's a lot of sideways too. His name really suits him. It flashed into his mother's brain when she first set eyes on him as a baby. After she had stopped screaming. Until that moment, she had been going to call him Trevor.

(Mrs Chunk, by the way, is the castle cook – and a very good one. She's had plenty of practice over the years, trying to keep up with her son's gigantic appetite. Not that she minds. She's proud of

Humperdump, now he's all grown up and the castle gaoler.)

The guardroom shows little sign of official business. It is kitted out as a kind of squalid leisure room, with an old mattress, a dartboard, and a small, greasy cooker with a blackened kettle on the top. There is a toppling pile of magazines in one corner – back issues of a monthly publication entitled *GOTCHA! Big pictures of handcuffs!* Humperdump gets it on subscription, which is paid for by his mum.

The only hint that this is the dungeon's business centre is the row of hooks hammered into the rough stone wall, on which are hung a number of rusty keys of varying sizes. These are mostly for show, as in fact there is a big, gleaming master key which opens pretty well everything. Humperdump personally takes care of this. It hangs on a ring which he always keeps close, together with another collection of useless keys, kept mainly for the jingle.

A heavy, partially opened door reveals a glimpse of stone passage. This is where the cells are. All six of them are empty.

Time to listen in.

'Any o' Mum's doughnuts left, Jimbo?' asked Humperdump, from his fleshy cave of hands. You would expect a man of his size to have a deep, hoarse, rumbling voice, but in fact it was surprisingly high and reedy.

'No, boss. You ate 'em all.'

This was Jimbo Squint, Humperdump's right-hand man. He was small and wiry, with shifty little eyes. Funnily enough, he *did* have a deep, hoarse voice. It was as though the pair of them had swapped. Right now, Jimbo was counting the spare keys on the wall and making notes on a clipboard. Humperdump and Jimbo solemnly counted the spare keys every day. It was a meaningless little ritual, but it filled in time and didn't involve heavy lifting.

'Did I? Funny, I don't remember.'

'That's the fing wiv comfort-eatin', though, ain't it, boss? You dunno yer doin' it. Shush, I'm countin' the keys. One – two – three –'

'What about the chocolate biscuits?'

'I fink you comfort-ate them too, boss. Four – five – six –'

'You see?' sighed Humperdump. 'That's what she's doin' to me. Makin' me eat without even knowin' I'm doin' it.' He slumped back in his chair, folded his arms and stared morosely at a puddle on the floor.

'Cheer up, it'll be time for yer second breakfast soon,' said Jimbo. 'She might come to the kitchens.

You might see 'er.'

There are two ways into the dungeons. You can go by way of a long corridor leading from the courtyard, involving a lot of keys and gates. The shorter way is via the kitchens, where Humperdump is frequently to be found tucking into vast, meaty meals provided by his mum, who feeds him on demand.

Humperdump has another reason for hanging about in the kitchens besides eating. He has his eye on Miss Fly. He loves everything about her – her hair, her nose, her shapeless cardigans, her screwed-up hankies, everything. He is forever hoping she will stop by for a bucket of fish heads for the cats, or a tray to take up to her room. Sometimes he is lucky – although she never stays long these days. Just scuttles in and scurries out again, not looking to right or left. Certainly not looking at him, even when he flirtatiously sticks his leg out.

To Humperdump's great disappointment, Miss Fly seems totally unaware of his deep interest. He has tried all the tricks he knows – ogling, leering, waving, winking, playfully tripping her up and so on – but for some reason, she isn't responding. So Humperdump is trying a new tack. He has begun sending her love notes. So far, he has sent four.

'You're sure you stuck the last note under the right

door?' he asked.

'I did, boss.'

'So why ain't she replied?'

'I dunno. Perhaps she's playin' hard to get. Maybe she ain't 'ad time to read it.'

'What about the others? She's had time to read them.'

'Maybe she's a slow reader. Maybe the cats ate 'em. Thirteen – fourteen –'

'She's breakin' my heart, Jimbo.'

'I know, boss. Fifteen – sixteen –'

'Is she doin' it on purpose, or what?'

'I dunno. Seventeen – eighteen –'

'She's the shinin' star in me thingy. The wind beneath me whatsits.'

'Eighteen – nineteen – twenty. That's it, all keys present and correct. Shall I write it in the book?'

'I don't care,' said Humperdump miserably. 'Do what you like. Why is she doin' this to me?'

'Cheer up, boss,' said Jimbo. 'Why don't you go and have a little lie-down on the mattress? Look at yer handcuff pictures?'

'I can't,' groaned Humperdump. 'I can't concentrate. I keep finkin' of 'er. Tryin' ter work out why she's ignorin' me. After all them notes.'

'What d'you say in 'em, boss? Them notes?'

'I puts I LUVS YOU. YORE HUMPY.'

'That's it?'

'Well – yer.'

'Ah, well, there's your reason right there. It's too short. You wanna be more flowery than that. Hearts 'n' flowers, that's what ladies like. You should write 'er romantic poems.'

'I dunno any.'

'So make one up. It can't be that difficult. Roses is red, grey is the sky, cowpats is greeny-brown an' I loves Miss Fly. Somethin' like that.'

Humperdump's mouth dropped open. 'Jimbo,' he said slowly, in awed tones. 'That is *beautiful*.'

'Oh, I dunno about *that* . . .'

'No, I mean it. However did you come up with it?'

'Ah, it's easy,' said Jimbo modestly, adding, 'Tell you what, boss. You can use it. My poem. Pretend you made it up yerself. 'Ow about that?'

'Really? Ah, fanks, Jimbo,' cried Humperdump excitedly. 'Give us a pencil, I'll do it right now!'

Just at that moment, there came an interruption. There was the noise of a faraway door crashing shut. Then the distant sound of slapping footsteps, followed by a sneeze. Then another crash. Then more footsteps, a bit nearer now. Then another sneeze.

'Oh my!' breathed Humperdump. 'I knows the sound o' them dainty little feet! It's 'er, Jimbo! *'Er!*'

The approaching feet were now slapping down stone steps.

'What shall I do?' panicked Humperdump. ''Ow do I look? Shall I stand up? Kiss 'er 'and? Go down on me knee an' propose? What?'

'Relax,' advised Jimbo. 'Stay in the chair, you look better sittin'.'

'But what'll I *say*?'

'Just be yerself, boss. Use yer natural charm. It's a bit soon to propose. Keep it light, be a bit playful. Ladies like that. Tease 'er a bit, make 'er blush.'

'Blush?'

The footsteps were slapping along the passageway now.

'Yeah. She'll probably tell you you're naughty an' slap yer arm, but she'll like it really. And compliment 'er on 'er hair. Ask after the cats. Offer 'er a drink. 'Ere she comes.'

Miss Fly came scuttling through the door. Her hair was on end, there were cobwebs all over her cardigan, and she had an anxious air. Her allergy is getting a serious grip. She can now no longer say her m's, her t's or her n's.

'Ah!' cried Miss Fly. '*There* you are, Chug. I've beed

lookig for you.'

'Oh ho ho,' said Humperdump teasingly, with a heavy wink to Jimbo. '*Have* you now? You little rascal.'

He waited for her to blush or playfully slap his arm. Instead, she fished in her pockets for a hanky, vigorously blew her nose, and demanded, 'Why are all the doors udlocked?'

'No point. No prisoners,' said Jimbo.

'The dudgeods are supposed to be locked ad all dibes.'

'Your hair,' said Humperdump. The flirtatious teasing hadn't done much, so he was moving on.

'Whad? Whad aboud id?'

'Your hair. It's all – wiggly.'

Miss Fly uneasily patted her cobwebby frizz and said, 'Yes. Well, I've beed up in the lofd. *Sub* of us have had a busy day.'

'I 'spect you been busy *readin'*, eh?' went on Humperdump meaningfully.

'Whad?'

'You know. The notes. You been readin' the notes.'

'Dodes? What dodes? I'b sure I dode dow aboud eddy dodes,' said Miss Fly stiffly. 'I've beed busy dealig with the cads.'

'I 'spect you cuddles 'em,' said Humperdump, seeing a fresh opening. 'Them cats. I 'spect you strokes 'em. Gives 'em hugs an kisses an' that. Tickles their tummies.'

'Well – yes.'

'I wish *I* was a cat,' said Humperdump. For him, this was serious courtship. Much more of this, and he'd be engaged. He looked over at Jimbo, who gave him a thumbs up.

'Fancy a drink?' went on Humperdump, encouraged. 'Sit down, finish my tea, I've only had a coupla slurps.'

'No thack you.' Miss Fly stared around. 'Eddyway, there's dowhere to sid.'

'Don't you worry,' said Humperdump. He patted his tree trunk thighs and wiggled his hairy eyebrows up and down. 'You can sit on my lap.'

'Certedly dod.' Hastily, Miss Fly backed away. 'This is dod a *social* call. I'b jusd here do ward you there is to be ad idspecshud.'

'Eh?' said Humperdump.

'Ad *idspecshud*. By her ladyship.'

'She means inspection, boss,' said Jimbo. 'That's torn it. I'll get the broom.' And he scuttled off.

'Why didn't you *say*?' cried Humperdump, heaving his vast bulk out of the chair. It took some time for his outer reaches to wobble to a halt. 'I gotta *change*! I gotta oil the manacles, swab out the cells, scrub off the graffiti, catch up on the paperwork, clear the place up. What time's she comin?'

Panic-stricken, he stared down at his filthy dungarees, licked his thumb and began rubbing at the worst of the stains.

'Now,' said a crisp voice from the doorway. 'She's coming now.'

Hastily, Humperdump wobbled to attention as Mesmeranza swept into the guardroom, high heels clicking. Tonight, she was dressed all in purple. Purple gown, purple evening gloves, everything purple except for the new red shoes.

'Evenin' m'lady,' croaked Humperdump. 'I didn't 'ear you comin'.'

'Evidently. You seem quiet down here, Chunk. I gather there are no prisoners, seeing you haven't bothered to lock any of the doors?'

'No m'lady. Fresh outa prisoners.'

'Well, I shall have to do something about that. I'm not paying you to *sit about*.' Mesmeranza stared around. 'Why is there an old mattress in here? What's the dartboard doing?'

'Just dumped temporarily. I bin meanin' to clear 'em out.'

'Why is there a filthy old cooker?'

'Jimbo makes 'imself a cuppa sometimes.'

'I suppose the mattress is his too, is it?'

'Yes.'

'Rubbish! You've been sleeping on the job again, haven't you? Sleeping and playing darts and sitting around drinking tea. On *my time*. Don't the pair of you ever do any work?'

'We been countin' the spare keys. I can show you the paperwork . . .'

'This guardroom is a slum. Wouldn't you agree, Fly?'

'I would,' said Miss Fly promptly. 'Id's shockig.'

Humperdump gave his beloved a hurt little glance. Miss Fly tightened her lips and said it again. '*Shockig.*'

'Follow me, Chunk,' said Mesmeranza, turning on her heel. 'I wish to inspect the cells. Bring a lantern.'

Humperdump seized a lantern from a hook on the wall and lumbered after her. Mesmeranza walked a few paces down the passageway, then stopped by the nearest cell. She ran a finger along the top bar. It came away filthy.

'See that?'

Humperdump said nothing. Mesmeranza stalked on, peering through the bars. Humperdump followed her, casting sad little glances over his shoulder at Miss Fly, who wouldn't meet his eye.

'When did you last change the straw?' demanded Mesmeranza.

'I dunno,' admitted Humperdump, scratching his head. 'Bin a while.'

'Well, I expect better than this. I have important things to do, demands on my time. I can't be expected to keep running down here to make sure you're doing your job. I've warned you before. No more slacking. I expect my staff to pull together as a team.'

'We will,' promised Humperdump. 'Me an' Jimbo, we'll get it sorted, I promise.'

'Do so. This is your last warning. And now I have other matters to attend to. I wish to inspect the cake. I take it the cake is ready, Fly?'

'Yes,' said Miss Fly. 'Jusd waidig for the icig to dry, Mrs Chug says.'

'Someone's birfday, m'lady?' asked Humperdump, trying to be sociable.

'Don't be ridiculous,' snapped Mesmeranza. 'What do I care about birthdays? The cake is part of the Plan. The Plan to get the cottage back.'

'Oh,' said Humperdump. 'Right. That.'

'Yes. *That*, as you say.'

'Mum said you was gearin' up to have another go.'

'Well, she was right. I am.'

'Haven't given up, then, m'lady?'

Mesmeranza reached up and grasped his big, red, hairy ear, which she pulled down to her level. 'Chunk,' she said. 'I *never* give up.'

Chapter Thirteen

Mrs Eckles Departs

It was two days later. Clover and Mrs Eckles stood at the garden gate, examining the donkey cart. It was a ramshackle affair, little more than a box on wheels with an old tarpaulin draped over a flimsy frame.

The donkey was ramshackle too. His back sagged in the middle. He had a scruffy coat with bald patches, large ears and soulful eyes. He fidgeted between the shafts, munching on a thistle.

'His name's Archibald,' said Mrs Eckles, stroking his nose.

'Well, he's certainly bald,' said Clover. Archibald flicked her a reproachful glance.

'Always takes me to the Fayre, don't you, Archie? Good as gold, he is. Run and get him a carrot, Clover.'

'Must I?' sighed Clover.

She was trying to keep out of the kitchen. Wilf was in there. He had been roped in to help out. It was his day off apparently. Actually, he was proving more of a hindrance. Right now, he was in the process of tying up boxes. He kept getting the string tangled, and had already cut his finger on the knife. Clover couldn't bear watching him.

'Go on. And don't let Wilf bring the boxful o' remedies, he'll drop it.'

'Right,' said Clover. And she trudged off back to the kitchen. So far, it had been a busy morning.

The previous day had been busy too, spent in a whirl of preparation for the trip. There was food to be cooked for a start. Clover had chopped, sliced, baked, fried, steamed and boiled, wrapping every-thing in neatly labelled little packages and packing them into an old wicker hamper. The rest of the time had been mostly spent in washing, ironing and mending Mrs Eckles' 'best' clothes. These consisted of an identical black frock and woolly shawl to the ones she always wore, but Mrs Eckles had pointed out that they didn't have so many holes. There were still quite a few, though, so Clover's sewing box was put to good use.

Clover hadn't mentioned the night-time incident. The business with the squeaky voice and the strange green light. It hadn't seemed quite so important when the sun was shining. When she had got up in the morning, she almost persuaded herself that she had dreamed it. Almost. Although Neville had certainly been in her room. There were muddy paw prints on the pillow.

She had gone down expecting to find the kitchen in turmoil, but in fact, it was looking quite respectable. Mrs Eckles had even washed up the supper dishes as promised. The only evidence that she had been working all night was the row of little jars and bottles lined up on the kitchen table. They had labels on, covered in her scrawly writing. *Purple Haze – 3 drops for the flux. Hairy Frogweed, for hevy swetin. Maiden's Hope – a spuneful on retirin. Swampgherkin. Waxwort. Dumblewater, Squiddik, Sloproot, Mambipamb.* Clover had never heard of any of them.

Mrs Eckles had certainly been busy. So busy that she had seemed inclined to take the day off, sitting on the garden bench with Neville in her lap, drinking tea, knitting the green blanket and watching Clover run about with baskets of washing and a mouthful of clothes pegs.

When night fell, she had announced that she was having an early night and vanished upstairs into her bedroom, leaving Clover to turn off the lamps, blow out the candles and lock the door. To Clover's relief, the second night had passed uneventfully. She was so tired she didn't even remember climbing into bed, let alone going to sleep.

And now it was the next day, and Mrs Eckles was off to the Fayre.

'She says don't touch the box with the jars in,' said Clover, entering the kitchen.

'All right,' said Wilf. 'I'll bring the hamper.'

He stooped down to pick it up, straightened, and cracked his head yet again on the low beam. Clover picked up the carrot and walked out quickly. There was something about the regularity of it all that was beginning to get on her nerves.

'What do you want me to do while you're gone?' she asked Mrs Eckles. She passed over the carrot and leaned on the gate, which seemed to be either asleep or sulking.

'That's up to you. You can knit a few rows of Neville's blanket, if you like. I ain't takin' it, won't 'ave time. Too busy rakin' the money in.'

'But I can't just sit and knit for three days.'

'Clean, then,' said Mrs Eckles, feeding carrot to Archibald. 'That's what you like doin', ain't it?'

'That won't take long. There's no one here to mess it up.'

'So do it yerself. Go mad. Wreck the place, then tidy it up again.'

'That's silly,' said Clover. 'I can't mess things up on purpose. It goes against my nature.'

'Ah,' said Mrs Eckles. 'Now, I can 'elp you there.'

Wincing, she bent down to the battered old carpet bag that lay at her feet. There came the clink of bottles as she rummaged around inside. Finally, she straightened. In her hand was a black corked bottle. She held it out to Clover.

'Here. Take three drops, as needed. No more, mind.'

'What is it?' Clover took the bottle and held it up to the light.

'Changeme Serum. It's a personality reverser. Whatever your nature is, it turns you into the opposite.'

'I see. I'm naturally tidy, but if I took this, I'd – what? Drop crumbs on the floor?'

'Ooh, a lot better than that. Go on a rampage o' mindless vandalism is more like it. The effects is quite dramatic.'

'And the point of that is?'

'No point. Just a bit o' fun.'

'Sounds like a waste of time,' said Clover.

'Go on, give it a go. It won't 'urt you.'

'I'd sooner make a start on the front garden.'

'Suit yerself. But stick it in yer pocket, just in case you changes yer mind. The effects only lasts an hour. Then you goes back to normal and cleans up. You'd enjoy that part.'

'I think I'll pass,' said Clover, dropping the bottle into her apron pocket. 'But thanks anyway.'

Wilf came staggering down the path with the hamper.

'Ah,' said Mrs Eckles. ''Ere comes lunch. Straight in the cart, if you please, Wilf. Stand back, Clover, give 'im room. *Open, gate!*'

'Opening *now*!' barked the gate, all keen and efficient.

Clover stood back and it opened, allowing Wilf to lurch through. He tottered towards the cart and gave a heave. The bottom of the hamper snagged on the

tailboard, jerked out of his arms and tumbled into a nearby ditch. From inside came the sound of a plate breaking.

'He could do with a few o' them drops,' whispered Mrs Eckles, and chuckled.

Loading the cart took for ever. Mrs Eckles let Clover and Wilf do most of the work. She seemed to be taking an awful lot for three days. As well as the hamper, there was a small folding table, the cauldron, the broom, a saucepan, a teapot, cups and saucers, blankets, an oil lamp and a tiny tent to sleep in. The only thing she insisted on dealing with herself was the box of 'remedies'. Clover tried to help when she saw her puffing down the path with it, but she shooed her away.

'Volatile,' she gasped. 'Gotta be kept steady. Get away, I know what I'm doin'.'

Finally, though, it was all done. All the bags and boxes were in, and Mrs Eckles had kissed and hugged Neville so many times that he struggled out of her arms and fled into the forest.

'Right, then,' she said, climbing stiffly into the cart. 'I'm off. Don't forget what I told you, Clover. I've strengthened the protection spells. You'll be all right as long as you don't invite no one in.'

'I know,' said Clover. 'You told me. Loads of times.'

'Yes, well, it's important. There's a certain person that just might try 'er luck while I'm out o' the picture. It wouldn't be the first time. Wilf knows what I mean. Don't you, Wilf?'

'It was only an old woman selling tomatoes,' said Wilf. He sounded rather sheepish, Clover thought.

'So *she* said. I ain't so sure.' Mrs Eckles picked up the reins. 'Anyway, you shouldn't 'ave let 'er in the garden. No strangers on the premises. That's what I told you.'

'I thought the gate was supposed to weed out friends from enemies.'

'The gate's rubbish, we all knows that. Goin' on the scrap heap soon as I got the cash for a new one. Anyway, enough talk. Make sure you lock up the chickens properly, Clover. Don't let Neville stay out after dark. Best if you don't an' all.'

'All right,' said Clover.

'Oh! If any more o' them cakes arrive, take 'em in. And save me some.'

She clicked to Archibald, who instantly set off at a fast clop, keen to be off and away.

'Do come again,' called the gate rather bitterly.

Clover and Wilf waved until she was out of sight.

'Now what?' said Wilf.

'I'm going in to straighten up,' said Clover.

'Need any help?'

'No thanks. Haven't you got things to do?'

'Nope. It's my morning off. Any chance of a cuppa?'

Clover sighed. All she seemed to do was make tea.

Chapter Fourteen

The Serum

Mrs Eckles' departure had caused quite a bit of mess. There were footprints all over the floor, bits of string and dirty cups from the endless cups of tea she had consumed.

Wilf sat at the kitchen table, slurping tea and flipping up sugar lumps, while Clover bustled around tidying.

'I *do* wish you wouldn't do that,' she sighed as the third one bounced off his nose and fell on the floor.

'She's taken the broom. It takes ages to sweep up with the little brush.'

'Just practising,' said Wilf.

'Well, do it somewhere else. I've got work to do.'

'Like what?'

'I'm going to make a start on the front garden. Pull the weeds up and fish the frogs out of the well.'

Wilf stretched out his legs, sat back in his chair and whistled tunelessly for a bit. Then he said casually, 'What was that she was saying about drops?'

'Drops?'

'I heard what she said. When I dropped the hamper. She said I could do with a few drops. What drops?'

'It doesn't matter.'

'What drops?'

'Not important.'

'What drops?'

Clover gave a sigh.

'If you *must* know, she gave me a bottle of something called Changeme Serum. You take three drops and it turns you into the opposite of what you are. So she says.'

'What – so I'd turn into a fat boy with golden curls and tiny little ears?'

'No.' Clover gave a little giggle at the thought. 'I

don't think it changes the way you look. Just your nature. She reckons if I took it I'd stop caring about being tidy and go on a rampage. Start kicking things around, just for the fun of it. Personally, I think it's a silly idea.'

'Where is it?'

'In my pocket.'

'Let's see.'

'Why?'

'I just want to see what magic serum looks like, that's all.'

Clover took the bottle from her pocket and placed it on the table. Wilf reached out his hand.

'Don't touch it!' said Clover. 'I know you. You'll drop it.'

'Are you saying I'm clumsy?'

'Do wolves wee in the woods?'

'Hmm.' Wilf rested his arms on the table, studying the bottle. 'But I guess, if this stuff really works, I'd be the opposite. What's the opposite of clumsy?'

'Skilful? Graceful? Whatever it is you're not.'

'How long do the effects last?'

'An hour.'

'Hmm. A whole hour of being skilful and graceful. I'd like that.' His eyes had a certain thoughtful gleam.

At exactly the same time, they shot their hands out. Wilf got there first, because he was nearest.

'Aha!' he cried, snatching up the bottle, fumbling, nearly dropping it, then catching it again by accident.

'Give it back,' demanded Clover.

'No way,' said Wilf, uncorking it and sniffing. 'Oooh! It smells of aniseed.'

'I'm telling you, Wilf. Give it *back*.' Clover leaped towards him.

But she was too late. He held her at arm's length, at the same time shaking out three drops on to his tongue. He swallowed. Then he re-corked the bottle, popped it in his pocket, smacked his lips and said, 'Mmmmmm.'

'What does it taste like?' asked Clover, curious despite herself.

'Aniseed. Yum.'

'Well, it'd serve you right if it tasted awful. You had no right to do that.'

'Just listen to you,' said Wilf. 'You do go on.' He reached out his hand, selected a sugar lump and casually flipped it into the air, opening his mouth at the same time.

His ginger eyebrows shot up in shocked surprise as it cleared his teeth and plopped neatly on to his tongue. He crunched and swallowed.

'I did it,' he said wonderingly. Then a huge grin enveloped his face, and he shot up an arm, punching the air in triumph. '*Woo-hoo!* I did it! Did you *see* that?'

'Probably a fluke,' said Clover. 'Try again.'

Excitedly, Wilf took another lump and flipped it high into the air. It pinged against a rafter, deflected sideways, slid down a bunch of herbs hanging from a hook, and landed slap in the middle of his extended tongue.

'You see? *Tricks*, even! Admit it, you're impressed.'

'Actually,' admitted Clover, 'actually, I am.' She couldn't help smiling at his pleasure.

'Got anything fiddly you want doing?' Eagerly, Wilf leaped to his feet. For once, he didn't crack his head on the low beam. 'Come on, come on. Any needles you want threading? Clocks mending? Quick – I need to do something that requires a steady hand!'

He began running about the kitchen looking for things to demonstrate his new-found skills.

He snatched up a clothes peg and balanced it on the end of his nose. He spotted Neville's ball and dribbled it around the kitchen, still balancing the clothes peg. He grabbed two eggs out of the egg basket and began juggling them.

'See this? See? I'm an egg juggler!'

'Don't,' said Clover nervously. 'Just calm down, why don't you?'

But her eyes opened wide when he added a third. Then a fourth. Then a fifth. Then, unbelievably, a *sixth*! The air was full of flying eggs.

Clover put her hands over her face.

When she removed them, all the eggs were safely back in the basket. Much to her alarm, Wilf was now brandishing a large kitchen knife in one hand and an apple in the other.

'Here,' he said, holding out the apple. 'Stand still and put this on your head.'

'Not likely,' said Clover.

'I can do it, I know I can!'

'*No*, I said.'

'Get me some matches, then. I feel an urge to build a cathedral out of matchsticks.'

'No. You're not wasting matches.'

'No, no, all you say is no. What about a dance?'

'*What?*'

'Come on, I want to see if I can do it without treading on your toes!'

And before she knew it, he was expertly whirling her round the kitchen. He didn't tread on her toes once.

'You see?' he cried, twirling her to a halt. 'There's

nothing I can't do. I think I'll become a brain surgeon and give dancing lessons in my spare time.'

'You'll have to be quick,' said Clover, flushed and giggling a bit. 'It only lasts an hour, remember?'

'Then I'll take some more.'

'No, you won't. You'll give that bottle back right now.'

'Not unless you promise to try it.'

'Don't be so silly.'

'Come on, you've got to try it. It'll be fun. You can go on a rampage, and I'll dance gracefully in the ruins.'

'Wilf,' said Clover. 'Get this into your head. I'm *not* going to try the serum. I'm going to do some gardening. Give me the bottle. I'm going to put it upstairs, out of harm's way.'

'Aw, but –'

'*Now,*' said Clover firmly.

Reluctantly, Wilf reached into his pocket, took out the bottle and dropped it into her hand.

'You're such a spoilsport,' he sighed.

'Thank you,' said Clover. And she marched briskly towards the stairs.

'What can I do while you're gone?' shouted Wilf rather desperately.

'I don't know. I'm sure you'll find something to

amuse yourself.'

She ran up the stairs and along the landing, then climbed up the ladder into her room, which was uncomfortably hot and stuffy. Bottle in hand, she crossed over to the chest, opened the bottom drawer and carefully placed it next to her old, darned stockings. She shut the drawer, walked to the window and opened it wide, to let some fresh air in. Then she went back down again.

The whole thing had only taken a minute or two. But that was long enough.

Chapter Fifteen

The Secret of the Cottage

'Just what do you think you're doing?'

Wilf was standing in front of Mrs Eckles' private cupboard with his back turned, fiddling with something.

'Opening the cupboard. Hang on, I've nearly – ah! There. That's got it.' He turned around. In one hand was a small piece of wire. In the other was the padlock. 'There's no point in glaring, I've done it now.'

'Put it back on,' said Clover.

'No way.'

'Put it *back*.'

'Nope. I'm taking a look.'

And so saying, Wilf grabbed hold of the handle and pulled. The door opened, revealing . . .

Bare shelves. Nothing but empty wooden shelves with dust on. There were rings in the dust, made by the dozens of little jars which Mrs Eckles had taken with her.

'Well, would you look at that,' said Wilf. 'Talk about a disappointment. And there was I thinking . . . hang on a minute, though. There *is* something, right at the back of the top shelf.'

He reached in. When he withdrew his hand, he was holding a book. A thin book, covered in dust. He wiped it on his sleeve, and a black cover emerged. On it, in gold lettering, were the words: *Manuel For Cottage.*

Wilf opened it to the first page and frowned.

'There's writing. I don't know what it says. I can't read, can you?'

'A bit. Give it here.'

Clover bent over the page. There were a few short

lines of tiny, neat writing in the very centre. She flipped through the book. The rest of the pages were blank.

She turned back to the first page.

'What's it say?' urged Wilf.

'*Users of this ma-man-ual are ad-advised that all summon-ings will be ans-answered on a st-strictly first come, first served basis,*' read Clover slowly. '*If we are cur-rently unable to provide imm-ediate response, contact Cus-customer Services.*'

'What?' said Wilf.

'Don't ask me. There's a bit more. A poem, or something. Listen. *To summon, repeat the foll-owing words.*

> *Imp-et-us I lack*
> *And need the bubble.*
> *Arise and bring the sack*
> *Or you're in trouble.*

What an earth is that supposed to m—?'
BANG!
The noise was very sudden, and very loud, like a thunder crack. It was accompanied by an almighty flash of blinding green light and the smell of singed eyebrows. Wilf reeled back, arms windmilling to

keep his balance. Clover dropped the book and threw up her hands to protect her eyes.

When she took them away again, the kitchen was full of thick, green, luminous smoke. Lazily, it coiled in the air – and slowly drifted towards all four corners of the kitchen.

There was something – no, *someone* – in the cupboard.

A little man. A *really* little man. A little man who was so little, he could have fitted into a milk jug. He was standing slap bang in the middle of the central shelf, glaring out at them.

Everything about him was green. Green skin. Tiny green jerkin. Short green trousers, which ended at half mast well above his feet, which were bare and dirty, with horny green toenails. Bald green head and straggly green beard. His ears were large and green. His little green hands had webs between the fingers. Over his shoulder was a green sack.

There was a short, shocked pause.

'Crikey!' breathed Wilf, recovering. He moved forward and stood peering up at the shelf. 'What is it? A *gnome* or something?'

'*It?*' snarled the little green man. 'I'm an *it* now?'

Clover recognised the voice. It was the one she had heard speaking to Mrs Eckles. It had an irritable tone, like a clerk in the post office who has two more annoying customers to deal with before coffee break.

'I thought all gnomes were its,' said Wilf.

'I am not a gnome!'

'Pixie, then. Whatever. Where's your hat?'

'My *what*?'

'Pixies and gnomes wear little pointy hats. Everyone knows that.'

'Watch my lips, boy.' The little man leaned forward. 'I am not a pixie, gnome, fairy, sprite, elf, brownie, goblin, leprechaun or flibbertigibbet. I am –' he drew himself up to his full height, which frankly wasn't far – 'an *Imp*.'

'Fair enough,' said Wilf. 'But where's your hat?'

'*Imps don't wear hats!*'

'Sssh,' said Clover. 'You're making him annoyed.'

'Look at his little legs, though,' said Wilf, enraptured. 'Let's take him out and make him run round on the table!'

He reached out an eager hand. Clover briskly slapped it away.

'So what do we call you?' she enquired. 'Do you have a name?'

'Bernard,' said the Imp.

'Bernard?' cried Wilf. 'What kind of a name is that?'

'Mine,' said Bernard tightly.

'Well, it shouldn't be. Imps should have cheeky, jolly names. Jimminy or Trippetty or – I dunno, Blackberry Joe. Tommy Tippytoes. Mr Squeebles.'

'Not that,' said Clover. 'Mr Squeebles is silly.'

'Better than Bernard,' said Wilf. 'That's just not right.'

The Imp was scowling horribly. Clover felt she should intervene, before Wilf could say any more.

'There's nothing wrong with Bernard,' she said. 'It's a very nice name. Won't you tell us what you're doing living in Mrs Eckles' cupboard, Bernard?'

'I don't *live* in the cupboard. I've got a place of my own. I just answer the summons, do the job and go home.'

'What, to your little cave?' asked Wilf.

'That's dwarfs,' sneered Bernard.

'How does the summoning bit work?' asked Clover. 'How do you just – appear? In a puff of green smoke?'

'Let's just call it magic, shall we? Of course, I could tell you all about portal technology and enchantment theory and so on, but I won't because it would all go over your silly heads. Can we get on? I take it you've made up your minds?'

'About what?'

'The *destination*, of course. Come on, out with it. I've got a pork pie waiting at home.'

'Imps don't eat pie – *ow*!' said Wilf as Clover stepped on his toe. 'Well, they don't!' he protested. 'They live in mushroom houses and drink dew.'

'That's pixies,' snapped Bernard witheringly. 'Shows how much you know.'

'Well, I do know you ought to wear a pointy hat,' said Wilf, 'if you want to be taken seriously.'

'Look,' said Clover, glaring at him, 'forget about hats. Ignore him, Bernard, he's an idiot. What do you mean about the destination?'

'There you go again, asking me. I don't make the decisions. I'm just the operator. You should have sorted all this out already, you know. Just tell me where you want the cottage to fly, and –'

'*Fly?*' said Clover.

'*Fly?*' said Wilf.

They exchanged astonished glances. Together, they said, '*The cottage flies?*'

'Of course it *flies*!' said Bernard impatiently. 'It's a *flying cottage*. Didn't she tell you?'

No, thought Clover. She didn't. Why not? Couldn't she trust me?

'I've heard of flying carpets,' said Wilf, 'but I've never heard of flying cottages.'

'No? A clever boy like you? Who knows all about hats?'

'They're rare, aren't they?' asked Clover.

'Sadly, yes. Very few still operational these days. Gone out of fashion. Times change.'

'Do all flying cottages come with an Imp?'

'Of course. Imps provide the *imp*etus. If you don't know what that means, look it up.'

'How does it work?' asked Wilf excitedly. 'Does it sprout wings or something? Is there a magic word? What?'

'Oh my.' Bernard gave a heavy sigh. 'Such ignorance.' He shook his head, and tutted. When he spoke again, it was as though he was explaining how to tie laces to a toddler. '*You* say where you want to go. *I* float the bubble. *We* fly there.'

'What bubble?' asked Clover.

Bernard loosened the string of the sack he was holding. He reached in and produced a strange, wobbling, transparent object, about the size of a small apple. It trembled in his webbed hands, rather like a soap bubble. Carefully, keeping it steady, he held it out.

'Look inside. But whatever you do —' he glared at Wilf, 'don't touch.'

The bubble slowly wobbled to a trembling halt.

Inside was a minute replica of the cottage. Everything was there – front garden, back garden, cherry tree, gate, every last detail. Two little specks were moving around the lawn. The chickens. You needed good eyesight to spot them.

'It's the cottage,' breathed Clover.

'Oh, give the girl a prize.'

'I don't understand. Are *we* in there?'

'Of course. Everything is duplicated in miniature.'

'So – you're in there too? Talking to us?'

'Yes.'

'Can we fly *now*?' burst in Wilf. 'Right this minute?'

'Well, it's all very inconvenient, but if you insist I'm contractually obliged to take you.'

'So we could just – *whoosh off*?'

'I wouldn't say whoosh. Gets stiff after it's been grounded. The creepers anchor it down. There are sometimes a few small teething troubles on take-off. Once up, it should settle down.'

He sounded confident, but his eyes had a rather nervous flicker.

'How long since it – flew?' asked Clover.

'Seven years ago,' said Bernard promptly. 'Every seven years she gives it a stretch, to make sure everything's still in working order. Just a quick spin, over the forest and back again. She doesn't like to do it more often these days. She says it wrecks the garden and upsets the hens.'

'And nobody noticed a cottage flying over their heads?'

'It was night. Besides, once it picks up speed, it goes faster than the human eye can follow. From the ground, it looks like a shooting star. All part of the design. We're talking old magic here. Something you know nothing about.'

He's right, thought Clover. I don't. And it's probably best to keep it that way.

Wilf, of course, felt otherwise. His eyes were shining with excitement and he was running his fingers through his red hair.

'This is fantastic!' he croaked. 'Can we go anywhere?'

'Yes.'

'Wilf,' said Clover.

'What – anywhere in the *whole wide world*?'

'Yes. I said, didn't I?'

'Wilf,' said Clover again.

'Could we go to . . . Palsworthy Fayre? They say you can buy that fluffy pink candy stuff! I've always wanted to try –'

'*Wilf!*' shouted Clover. He broke off and looked at her.

'What?'

'We're not going anywhere. We're going to put the Imp away. No offence, Bernard.'

'Suits me,' said Bernard. Very, very carefully, he placed the bubble back in the tiny sack, pulled the drawstring and glared. 'Kindly don't bother me again. I don't like being called out on false pretences. Put the manual back where you found it and shut the door behind me. Time-wasters!'

And with that, he vanished. Just like that. No bang. No more smoke. The cupboard was empty.

'Well,' said Clover. 'I hope you're pleased with yourself. Poking around in things that don't concern you.'

Crossly, she picked up the thin black book from the floor, where it had fallen.

'Ah, but I couldn't help it, could I? It was the serum. The padlock was just crying out to be picked.'

'You weren't supposed to drink the serum either. She gave it to me, not you.'

Clover stood on tiptoe, put the book back on the top shelf, shut the cupboard door and snapped the padlock on the latch.

'There. Don't touch it again.'

'All right. No need to be so bossy.'

'Or for you to be so nosy. It's all very well for you.

I've got to sleep here tonight, knowing I'm in a flying cottage with an Imp called Bernard in the cupboard.'

'He's not in the cupboard. You heard him. He's gone home to Imp Land to eat pie.'

'And that's what I'd like you to do.'

'I haven't got a pie. We're having pancakes.'

'I mean go home. You've caused enough trouble for one day.'

Clover stood with her hands on her hips, waiting.

'All right,' said Wilf. He still lingered, though. 'You're sure you'll be OK? Staying here on your own?'

'I'll be fine.'

'I'll come round first thing tomorrow morning. On my way to the shop.'

'What, to try and sneak more serum? Or break into the cupboard again and get Bernard to fly you off on a nice little outing somewhere?'

'No. To check you're all right.'

'Oh.' Clover felt a bit guilty. 'Well, I suppose so, if you must.'

Wilf moved towards the door, then paused and looked back at her.

'The cottage flies,' he said wonderingly.

'Yes.'

'I can't get my head around that.'

'No. Can we just stop talking about it now?'

Wilf shook his head, then slowly wandered off into the sunlit garden – but not before he had stumbled over the step. Evidently, the serum was wearing off.

Clover stood where she was for a moment or two, watching the last faint tendrils of green smoke drift out the door.

So. She was standing in a cottage that flew. No wonder Mrs Eckles said it was special.

She shook her head and went to find the shears. It was time to do a bit of sensible gardening. She'd had enough magic for one day.

Chapter Sixteen

Mesmeranza Prepares

And now we must move on a few hours. We are back in Castle Coldiron. Somewhere behind the thick grey clouds, the sun is setting. Light is draining from the sky. Soon it will be dark. Night comes quickly in the mountains.

Where is Mesmeranza? What is she doing?

She is in the dining room, inspecting a collection

of items assembled at one end of a long, polished table. Tonight, she is all in red. Red gown, a red feather in her hair and, of course, the red shoes. A large red handbag dangled from her wrist.

The dining room is lit by dusty chandeliers. Several have lost their crystals, and don't look very nice close up, although they give a good effect from a distance. There is a long crack running across the ceiling. The wood panelling is chipped here and there. What the room needs is a good old facelift, just like the rest of the castle, but it won't get it. Not tonight, anyway. More important things are afoot.

The items on the table have been searched for, found, gathered together, carted up and down long corridors and many flights of stairs and finally laid out on the table by Miss Fly, who is still gasping from the effort. Her allergy is even worse. She has developed a cold sore, and can't say her m's, t's, n's or p's. Even her c's have gone missing. In fact, she may well require a translation.

The items laid out on the table are as follows:

A pair of green glasses. We have seen these before, and in action.

A plain, black, deceptively innocent stick, pointed at one end, rather like an extra-long chopstick.

A furled umbrella, also black, with little lightning bolts carved on the handle.

A large, empty space.

Then, finally — a cake. A wonderful-looking cake, sitting resplendent on a plate fringed with a paper doily. It is covered in white sugar icing and tied with a red bow. There is a single, succulent red cherry placed perfectly in the very centre.

'Mrs Chunk has excelled herself,' said Mesmeranza. 'The cake is magnificent. At least one person does their job properly in this castle. I take it that's the Poncho?' She pointed to the empty space between the umbrella and the cake.

'Yes,' said Miss Fly. 'Id is.'

Mesmeranza wiggled her fingers in the space. 'Where?'

'Oh doh! Id was here a biddid ago. Id musd have slibbed dowd.' (Oh no! It was here a minute ago. It must have slipped down.)

Miss Fly scuttled forward and began batting at thin air. Then she bent down and peered under the table.

'Hurry up,' said Mesmeranza.

'I'b lookig. Id's by doze, I cad breed.' (I'm looking. It's my nose, I can't breathe.) Face flushed, gasping for breath, Miss Fly staggered upright and clutched at the table. 'I've god all dizzy. I cad bed doud.' (I've gone all dizzy. I can't bend down.)

'So? Don't expect *me* to look – you lost it. Stick your foot out, it can't have gone far.'

Miss Fly stuck out a tentative foot and waved it about. Suddenly, the tip of her hairy brown shoe vanished, as though cut off.

'Ah. Here id is.'

Wiping her nose, she stooped again, reached under the table and fumbled around. Suddenly and unexpectedly, both her arms disappeared below the elbow. She straightened, bent over the table, and they appeared again.

'There,' she wheezed.

The space still looked like a space, but now it smelt faintly of mothballs.

'I suppose I should try it on, just to be sure. Turn around, and don't look until I tell you.'

Obediently, Miss Fly turned her back. There was a short pause. Then . . .

'All right, you can look now. Tell me what you see.'

Miss Fly turned round. She was staring at empty space. Apart from a pair of feet, that is. A pair of solid feet, wearing the red-heeled shoes.

'I cad see your feed,' said Miss Fly. 'Id's a bid shord.' (I can see your feet. It's a bit short.)

'Really? That's a nuisance. Of course, I am taller than Grandmother. I'll try bending at the knees. How's that?'

'I cad still see theb. Try pullig id dowd bore.' (I can still see them. Try pulling it down more.)

'It won't pull down more, not with the hood up. If I put that down, you'll see my *head*, won't you?'

'You could wear flad shoes,' suggested Miss Fly.

'Don't be ridiculous,' said Mesmeranza coldly. 'I've already explained about these shoes, Fly. They are new and wonderful and I intend to wear them, even with a Poncho. *Especially* with a Poncho. I must retain some semblance of glamour. Oh, the beastly thing's so scratchy, I must take it off.'

Miss Fly watched in fascination as, with a rippling effect, an expanse of red robe materialised, up as far as the waist. Mesmeranza's top half was still non-existent. Then, slowly, the rest of her body appeared. There came the sound of muffled cursing. Her arms – rather unnervingly lacking hands – waved around at shoulder level, as she struggled to tug the invisible garment over her head.

Finally, the head appeared, looking hot and bothered, with the hair in some disarray.

Mesmeranza dumped the Poncho on the table, and the last missing bits – her hands – reappeared. 'What time is it?'

'Sevvud o'clog,' said Miss Fly, adding pointedly, 'the cads' subber tibe.' (Seven o'clock. The cats' supper time.)

'The cats can wait. I haven't finished with you yet. There are things I need you to do.'

'There are?' moaned Miss Fly wretchedly.

'Yes. This is the Big Night, Fly. I do wish you would enter more into the spirit of things. Go down to the stables and tell the groom to prepare Booboo. He'll need his Special Saddle. Total invisibility for both of us is essential for the first part of the venture. The Umbrella can go in the saddlebag and I'll keep the Hypnospecs in the Poncho pocket. I'll have to hold the cake on my lap and shield it as well as I can with the sleeves. And I'll wear *this* around my neck, on a string.'

Mesmeranza picked up the black stick, gave it a little shake and held it to her ear.

'Grandmother's Wand,' she mused. 'They don't make them like this any more. Plenty of charge left,

I can hear it humming. It's almost as though it's alive. All ready and waiting to unleash a mighty blast of power on the next unfortunate victim. What are you hanging about for, Fly? Go and tell Mrs Chunk to bring supper. I shall eat now, before I ride out.'

'Alride. Eddythig else?'

'Yes,' said Mesmeranza. 'Blow your nose.'

Miserably, Miss Fly trailed from the room.

The moment the door closed, Mesmeranza set the Wand back on the table. She picked up a chair, moved it directly in front of the cake, and sat down. She opened her bag and took out a small hand mirror and a pair of silver tweezers. She brought the mirror close to her face.

'Ooh!' squealed the mirror, apparently a tiny chip off the old block. 'How lovely you look tonight!'

'Shut up,' snapped Mesmeranza. 'I need to concentrate.'

The hand mirror lapsed into silence. Very carefully, without blinking once, she tweezed out a single eyelash.

She stretched out a hand and plucked the cherry from the cake. Holding the eyelash between finger and thumb, she placed it in the dent left in the snowy

expanse of icing. Then she replaced the cherry on top.

'There,' she breathed, eyes gleaming with satisfaction. '*That* should do the trick.'

Down in the castle kitchens, Humperdump Chunk sat slumped at the table, head once again in his hands.

'I don't fink she loves me, Mum,' he groaned.

'There, there,' said his mother soothingly. ''Course she does, Humpy. Fine figure of a man like you.'

'But she never stuck up for me in front of 'er ladyship. She made fings worse. It's like she wanted me to get in trouble.'

Mrs Chunk placed a huge, steaming plate before her lovestruck son.

'There, son. Get that down you. Roast turkey with all the trimmings. Your favourite.'

Humperdump picked up a fork and got stuck in.

'Didn't even reply to me love notes,' he sniffed, through a mouthful of roast potato.

'I'm sure there's a reason, Humpy. She's probably a bit shy, that's all.'

'That's what Jimbo said,' said Humperdump.

'You see? Give it another try, son. She'll come round.'

'You're right,' said Humperdump. 'Soon as I've mucked out the dungeon, I'll write 'er another one. Give 'er one more chance. Jimbo said he'd help. Any more gravy?'

Chapter Seventeen

A Strange Tale

Night was falling in the forest, and Wilf was making pancakes.

Pancakes were a big treat for Wilf and Grampy. It wasn't often that they managed to get hold of the basic ingredients. But tonight, they had. Well, Wilf had. The hens had both laid an egg a record six days in a row, and instead of eating his he had secretly saved them. There was a bit of flour in the cupboard – not much, but enough. And there was a tiny knob of butter.

Of course, after the excitement of the day, making pancakes wasn't quite as thrilling as usual – but Grampy would be surprised at any rate.

After leaving the cottage (the *flying* cottage!), Wilf had made a detour to Tingly Bottom to pick up his weekly three pence from Old Trowzer. He blew half of it on a twist of sugar, a lemon and a jug of milk, none of which he had got at a discount, despite being an employee. He had somehow managed to get everything home without mishap, despite the fact that his miraculous new skills had deserted him.

Cooking was always a hazardous occupation for Wilf, and tonight was no exception. He was finding it hard to concentrate. So far, he had dropped the frying pan on his foot, broken one of the precious eggs on the floor, spilled flour on his shirt, rubbed the skin off his hand when using the lemon grater and briefly set fire to his shorts.

Back to the old routine, he thought, patting his smoking rear, sucking his skinned hand and sadly staring around at the carnage. It was really horrible to go back to being his old clumsy self again, after that wonderful, fun-filled hour spent under the influence of the Changeme Serum.

Still. He had made the batter. It was rather lumpy, and not quite as much as he had hoped, after the accidents with the egg and the flour – but there was enough for two pancakes each.

He stood over the frying pan, watching the butter melt. The candles were lit and two clean(ish) plates were laid on the table. Now all he needed was Grampy. The firebox was nearly empty, which meant he was probably out gathering wood. He would be pleased to find everything ready to go. Well, perhaps not exactly *pleased*, because showing pleasure wasn't something Grampy did. But, hopefully, less grumpy.

The shack was a very basic affair. It consisted of one room in which Wilf and Grampy sat, slept, cooked and ate. Neither of them did much housework, because neither of them cared about that sort of thing. The few sticks of furniture were falling apart, but they had learned to live with that. They just avoided sitting on the worst of the collapsing chairs and remembered not to lean on the wobbly table, which sent your supper scooting into your lap if you weren't careful.

The door opened, and Grampy walked in. He was tiny and shrivelled, with a bald head and big, flapping ears. He wore a grubby collarless shirt and his trousers were held up with string. His mouth was collapsed inwards, because as usual, he hadn't bothered to put his teeth in. There was no sign of any firewood.

Wilf waited for the usual greeting. It could be one of several. Either 'Bloomin' parky out there!' or 'What's that muck yer cooking?' or 'What's that smell? You set fire to summat again?'

Tonight, none of them were forthcoming. Grampy looked – unsettled, somehow. A bit pale. Not quite himself.

'All right, Grampy?' asked Wilf. He waited for the response. Typically, this would be, 'Nah, bloomin' freezing. What you let the fire go down for?'

But it didn't happen. In silence, Grampy sank into his old easy chair.

'Not much kindling around? Never mind. I'm making pancakes. That'll cheer you up.' Wilf picked up the ladle and turned to the bowl of lumpy batter. 'I'll do yours first. I think you'd better toss it, or it'll end up stuck on –'

'Wilf,' interrupted Grampy, 'I know I'm gettin' on in years, but tell me the truth, lad. Am I goin' bonkers?'

'No. No, of course not, Grampy. Why?'

'It's just that – well, I think I might be seein'

things. Hearin' things. Things what ain't there.'

'Like what?'

'Like . . .' Grampy hesitated, then came out with it. 'Like . . . a phantom horse.'

'A phantom *horse*?'

'Aye.'

'I haven't seen any of those around lately,' said Wilf carefully. He put down the ladle and moved the frying pan away from the flame. 'Um – what makes you think *you* did?'

'Well,' said Grampy slowly. 'I was out gatherin' wood, close by old Mother Eckles' cottage. She don't like me doin' it, but I reckoned I was safe with her bein' away at the Fayre. That's what *you* told me, although I noticed there was a light in the window, so somebody must be there.'

'Clover,' said Wilf.

'Who?'

'Clover Twig. She's looking after the cottage.'

'What, Jason Twig's eldest? The sensible one?'

'That's her.'

'Good choice. Well, anyway. I gets a good armful an' I starts comin' back along the track, and all of a sudden I hears horse's hooves. A big blighter, it sounds like. Comin' towards me at a fast lick. All the little stones is jumpin' about on the track. Then it passes by, close as you are to me. So close, I can hear it snortin'. Big, hot, horsey breaths they was. But . . .' Grampy cleared his throat. 'No horse.'

'What?'

'You heard. I can hear it, I can feel its breath, but I can't see it. It carries on past me down the track a bit. Then it slows down, right? And I hears what sounds like someone dismountin'. But there still ain't nothin' there.'

'Probably your ears playing tricks,' said Wilf. 'When the wind's in the wrong direction, you can often hear things that *sound* close, but really –'

'That ain't all,' said Grampy. 'Know what I hears next? The sound of a hand slappin' the horse's rump. And know what I sees? I sees the branches of the trees movin', first low down, then higher up. Like there's somethin' big risin' from the ground and – kinda pushin' 'em apart, passin' through 'em. Terrible smashin' noises, twigs an' leaves rainin' down.'

'Well, like I say, the wind often –'

'Nothin' to do with the wind.' Grampy waved him quiet with an irritable hand. 'It was the *horse that wasn't there*. It was takin' off into the air. That's what I saw an' that's what I heard. And there's more.'

'There is?'

'Aye. The horse has gone, right?'

'How d'you know it's gone? It might have been parked above your head,' Wilf sniggered. 'You'd never know, unless it did a dirty great big invisible p—'

'Are you gonna carry on bein' clever, because if you are . . .'

'No, no, sorry, sorry. Go on. Then what?'

'The horse is gone. Everythin's quiet again. And then – then I sees summat else.'

'What?'

'Shoes,' said Grampy. 'A pair o' red shoes. Shoes with feet in 'em. Walkin' off down the path, back towards Mother Eckles' place. All by themselves. Daft, strappy things with dirty great heels. And you know what? You won't believe me, but floatin' above the feet is a cake. A bloomin' great fancy iced cake with . . . Wilf? What the . . .? *Wilf!*'

He was too late. Wilf was gone.

'Neville?' called Clover. 'Come on, Neville, where are you?'

She stood at the kitchen door with the biscuit tin, peering out into the moonlit garden. The stars were out, and there was no sign of any clouds. The chickens were safely in the coop, making comfortable little clucking noises. Now all she had to do was get

Neville in, and she could bar the door and settle down for the night. Make a last hot drink, maybe knit a row or two of the green blanket and retire to bed.

'Neville? Hurry up!' Impatiently, she rattled the tin.

No sign.

Clover was undecided. Mrs Eckles had been very clear about making sure Neville was in after dark. Should she go and look for him? It was a fine night, but somehow, she didn't want to step out into the still, silent garden.

She remembered Mrs Eckles' words.

Sometimes when I'm out in the garden. I can feel 'er watchin' through the Crystal. She's probably watchin' now.

A small breeze blew up, sending the cherry blossom whirling like dark snow. Clover gave a little shiver.

'*Neville!*' she shouted. '*You have to come in right now!*'

To her great relief, there was a rustle down by the bench and a familiar shape came strolling across the lawn, pausing every so often to spit out feathers.

'There you are! I've been calling for ages!' scolded Clover. 'Come on, then, let's go in. I want to get the door bolted.'

Things felt much better inside. Clover stared with pride around the cosy kitchen. Everything was neat and tidy, just as she liked it. The curtains were drawn, the fire flickered, the lamps glowed. The private cupboard was firmly padlocked and it felt – safe. Neville twined in and out of her legs, making it clear that the bird was just a snack and he was more than ready for the main course.

She gave him a bowl of milk and a handful of biscuits, which he disposed of in double quick time. Stifling a yawn, she poured the last of the milk into a saucepan and set it on the stove, then flopped tiredly into Mrs Eckles' rocking chair. It had been another long day.

Neville thumped up on to her lap.

'It's funny, isn't it? On our own,' said Clover, stroking his matted fur as she waited for the milk to heat. 'But we're all right, aren't we? The night'll soon be over. Tomorrow I'm going to carry on with the front garden. I'll have to pop into Tingly Bottom, because we're out of milk. Or ask Wilf to deliver some.'

The fire suddenly spat, making her jump. The clock ticked. Neville purred and drooled. His eyes were lazy slits.

'We're all right,' said Clover again. 'Nothing to

worry about. Nothing at all . . .'

There came a noise from outside. A footstep.

Neville froze. His purr cut off, and every bit of him went absolutely rigid. His eyes were now huge yellow circles. They were fixed on the door.

Clover's heart skipped a beat. Her mouth went very dry. Somebody was outside! She could hear faint rustling noises, and an odd little scraping sound.

'Who's there?' she called sharply. 'Is that you, Wilf?'

There was a pause. And then – then came three little knocks on the door. Timid little knocks, with a pause between them. They sounded – shy. Polite. Humble.

Tap. Tap. Tap.

She stood up, spilling Neville from her lap. He growled, deep in his throat, slowly backed away, then turned tail and fled up the stairs.

Clover walked to the stove and turned off the milk. Then she went to the kitchen window. Taking a deep breath, she grasped the curtain, wrenched it open, pressed her nose to the glass and peered out into the garden.

All was still. No movement, except for a few silvery blossoms drifting down from the cherry tree.

Nobody stood on the doorstep.

There was something else, though.

A cake. A magnificent cake, covered in white sugar icing with a large red cherry in the middle, tied with a red ribbon and spectacularly lit by the moon.

Clover went weak with relief.

'It's just another cake, Neville,' she called. 'Come on down, you scaredy-cat.'

But wherever Neville was, he was apparently happy to stay there.

Clover stood at the window, debating what to do. She didn't particularly want to undo all the bolts again, now the cottage was all safely tucked up for the night. But it was such a beautiful cake. Supposing the squirrels got at it, or the birds? She really ought to bring it in and put it in the pantry.

Still, she hesitated.

It was at that point that a large black cloud slid across the moon. The garden went from silver to black. And then it began to rain. Slowly at first, just a thin pitter-patter of drops. Then heavier. Within seconds there was a downpour.

That did it. Clover dropped the curtain and hurried to the door. If she left the cake out, it would be ruined. Anyway, what was she afraid of? It wasn't as though she had to cross the threshold. She could just reach out and bring it in.

It only took a moment or two to deal with the locks and bolts.

Chapter Eighteen

Surprise!

Outside, the rain was really lashing down. Heavy drops were bouncing off the cake and rapidly forming a puddle on the doorstep. Hastily, Clover reached out and picked it up – it was satisfyingly heavy – then moved back into the kitchen.

Behind her, a sudden gust of squally wind tore the door wide open, then smashed it closed again. The candles flickered in the freezing draught.

The cake smelled wonderful – of sugar and spice

and all things so unbelievably nice that she made up her mind to cut a slice and have it with her hot milk. She carried it to the table, admired it for a moment, then hurried back to deal with the bolts.

There, she thought, as she shot the last one across. Safe again.

Outside, the rain stopped abruptly. Just like that.

'Neville?' shouted Clover. 'Where are you?' She went to the staircase and peered up into the shadows. There was no sign of him.

'Come on down,' she coaxed. 'If you're really good I'll give you a little lick of icing.'

And a voice in her ear said, 'Well. Isn't *he* the lucky cat?'

Clover whirled round and nearly collapsed with shock.

Floating in the air just behind her was a head.

It was a woman's head. The hair was swept up in an elaborate pile that reached almost to the rafters. Perched on top of the hair was a pair of large glasses with green frames. The face beneath was powdered white – all but the mouth, which was scarlet. The eyes were emerald green. Identical eyes to Mrs Eckles' – except colder. Harder.

The head was abruptly cut off at the base of the neck. Floating in the air some way below was a furled, dripping umbrella – and at floor level, there was a pair of feet, jammed into a pair of bright red high-heeled shoes.

Slowly, the disembodied feet backed towards the door, with the head keeping pace. The hard green eyes never left Clover's face. The umbrella rose and deposited itself on the hook where Mrs Eckles always hung her pointy hat.

There was a rustling sound, and a body began to emerge. It appeared with a kind of confused rippling effect, one bit at a time. First, the ankles. Then the lower part of a scarlet gown. Then two arms materialised, wearing matching scarlet elbow-length gloves. Then came the upper part of the body – then the shoulders. The head vanished briefly, then was back again, joined to the neck. There was the sound of something wet and woolly dropping to the floor.

'Surprise!' hissed Mesmeranza.

Clover's eyes flickered to the drawer containing the rolling pin.

'I'd advise you not to try anything stupid,' went on Mesmeranza. 'I'm in, you see. In at last. Back in the dear old cottage. And about to make myself at home.'

She stooped down – and both hands vanished.

She reached up to the hook and, suddenly, her hands were once again on the end of her arms.

'There,' she said. 'Know the old saying? Wherever I hang my Poncho of Imperceptibility, that's my home.'

'No it isn't,' said Clover, finding her voice at last.

'I beg your pardon?'

'It's wherever I hang my *hat*. That's Mrs Eckles' hook. She hangs her hat there. That makes it *her* home.'

'Not any more,' said Mesmeranza. 'I'm over the threshold. All spells are down, all bets are off, all old folk sayings are rubbish anyway and the cottage is mine.'

Suddenly, with no warning, she threw open her arms and twirled around on the spot.

'Mine!' she shrieked. 'Mine mine *mine*!'

Then she began to laugh. It was a shrill, triumphant cackle that went on for quite a long time. Clover thought it was overdone.

'Have you quite finished?' asked Clover. 'If you must gloat, at least do it quietly.'

Mesmeranza spun to a halt. She put her head on one side and examined Clover.

'Oooh! Big, bold words from such a small girl! It's not a good idea to clash with *me*, dearie. Do you know who I am?'

'Oh yes. I know,' said Clover. 'You're Mrs Eckles' sister. She's told me a lot about you.'

'Oh, she has? Like what?'

'Well now, let me think. What was it again? Oh yes. You're greedy. And selfish and vain and spiteful and never want to share. Shall I go on?'

'Please do,' said Mezmeranza dangerously.

'You're unkind to animals. And you're not even good at witchcraft, because you need a load of silly *stuff* before you can even work a tiny spell. Oh, and you cheat.'

'I *do*?'

'Yes. You're as old as she is. You only look like that because you've got the Mirror of Eternal Youth.'

'I see. She told you about that, did she?' Mesmeranza spoke coldly. Her green eyes narrowed. 'Anything else?'

'Yes. She said you can't come in unless you're invited.'

'Well,' said Mesmeranza, 'that just goes to show how wrong she is. Because, would you believe it, here I am! And do you know what? It's *your* fault. You brought me in. Well, not all of me. Just a small *piece* of me. An eyelash, to be precise. A single

204

eyelash, hidden in the cake, that's all it took. And the second you brought it over the threshold, the rest of me followed wearing Grandmother's trusty Poncho.'

'You should let it down,' said Clover. 'It shows your silly feet. And it smells of mothballs.'

'I don't think you're in a position to make personal remarks, miss,' snapped Mesmeranza. 'That green dress is *very* faded, and the boots are simply appalling. Who are you anyway? Do you have a name?'

'Clover Twig. I'm here to clean. I'm taking care of the cottage while Mrs Eckles is away.'

'Well,' said Mesmeranza, staring around, 'I can see you're a good cleaner. I've never seen the old place looking so thoroughly scrubbed. But you've fallen down rather badly in the caretaking department, I'm afraid. So I shall fire you.'

'You can't do that,' said Clover.

'And why is that?'

'Because you didn't hire me. Mrs Eckles did.'

'Mrs Eckles, Mrs Eckles! It might have escaped your notice, but Demelza is conspicuous by her absence. I'm in charge now, and very much looking forward to settling in.'

Mesmeranza gave a little twirl, then threw herself

into Mrs Eckles' rocking chair.

'You see?' she purred. 'Here I am, making myself comfortable. In a moment, I shall treat myself to a celebration slice of that delicious cake. And then I shall reacquaint myself with the old place. Drag the wretched cat out from wherever he's hiding and tie his whiskers in knots, just like I did in the old days. Poke around in private cupboards and help myself to anything I fancy. Unravel Demelza's knitting. And then, finally, when I'm good and ready, off I shall go, taking the cottage with me. Sadly, my plans don't include you. You, little Miss Twig, will be going home.'

'So make me.'

The words were out before Clover could stop them. They were probably not very wise words but, as we know, Clover has a stubborn streak.

'Oh, I can *make* you. Nothing will give me more pleasure.' Mesmeranza reached up, took the dark glasses from her head and settled them on her nose. 'Look into the glasses. Look deep. What do you see?'

'Little green sparks,' said Clover. She shifted her eyes very slightly until she was focusing on Mesmeranza's nose. Then she disconnected her brain from her eyes. The sparks whizzed about

angrily, demanding her attention, dancing on the edge of her vision, but Clover ignored them. She was thinking about other things.

'Are they spinning?'

'Yes,' said Clover. She was thinking frosty mornings, when you could see your breath in the air.

'You're under. Listen to my voice. You will leave this cottage. You will walk straight home and you will not return. You will tell nobody about this meeting. What did I just say?'

'That I've got to go home, not come back and say nothing,' said Clover, thinking about the taste of ripe cheese.

'Good,' said Mesmeranza. There was a long pause. 'Well, go on, then.'

'No,' said Clover, thinking about what everyone would be doing at home right now. 'I like it where I am, thank you.'

'Why aren't you under?' snapped Mesmeranza. She snatched off the glasses. 'How are you able to resist the Hypnospecs? Has Demelza been training you up? Is that it?'

'No,' said Clover. 'I'm just good at staring.'

'Oh, you are? Then it seems that tougher measures are required. Let's see how good you are at dealing with *this*!'

She pulled at the string around her neck. Hanging on it was a thin black stick. She raised her arm and pointed it at Clover.

'Goodbye, Clover Twig,' she said. 'I doubt we'll meet again.'

And then the world exploded.

Chapter Nineteen

Breaking and Entering

Wilf was only a short way away from the cottage when he saw the flash. A sudden vivid blue-green blaze of light that briefly lit the trees ahead, then flickered out.

Panting hard, trying to move quietly and not to bump into anything, he crept forward, keeping low and ducking behind bushes. He stopped behind a tree at the edge of the moonlit glade and cautiously peered around.

There were no lights showing in the cottage. It looked just the same as it always did . . . apart from one thing. The gate was off its hinges. It lay flat on the ground. It had a nasty dent in its bottom bar, and it wasn't talking.

'Pssssssst!' hissed Wilf. 'Gate!'

There was a pause. Then a little tinkling sound, like rust falling. And the gate said feebly, 'Out of order. Try again tomorrrr . . .'

Its voice rattled off into silence.

'Wilf?'

The voice came from out of the darkness. He whirled around. There, sprawled on the ground, half in and half out of a ditch, was Clover. She looked quite unlike herself. Her dress was crumpled. There were twigs and leaves in her hair, and her face was very pale.

'Clover!' gasped Wilf. 'Are you all right? What happened?'

He hurried towards her and stretched out a hand. Uncertainly, she grasped it and he hauled her to her feet.

'I don't know exactly,' said Clover. 'One minute I was in the kitchen, then she pointed the Wand at me and . . . Whoo! I feel a bit dizzy.'

'She?' Wilf put an arm around her shoulders to steady her.

'Mesmeranza! Mrs Eckles' horrible sister! She's taken over the cottage! I did my best, but I couldn't stop her.'

'Of course you couldn't,' said Wilf soothingly. 'It wasn't your fault.'

'But it is! I took the cake in! I wasn't going to, but she used the Bad Weather Umbrella and I thought it'd get ruined in the rain. She must have been waiting by the door, but I didn't see her because she was wearing the Poncho of Imperceptibility . . .'

'Whoah!' said Wilf. 'Look, just slow down. Let's move back under the trees.'

Firmly, he led her into the shadows. There was a fallen branch, and he gently pushed her down on to it, then crouched next to her.

'Just take a deep breath and tell me everything.'

'Well,' said Clover, 'I was sitting in the kitchen . . .' And she told him all about it, in as few words as possible.

'Well, I'm blowed,' said Wilf grimly when she finished. 'An eyelash, eh? Talk about sneaky.'

'But I should have been more careful. I should have guessed it was a trick.'

'I don't see how. Mrs Eckles said cakes were all right. You weren't to know.'

'That doesn't help, though, does it?' said Clover miserably. 'I let her in. She's going to steal the cottage and it's all my fault and I don't know what to do.'

'*We*, you mean. We're in this together.' This sounded rather brave and heroic, so he repeated it. 'Yes, we're definitely in this together. You can count on me.'

'What are you doing here anyway?' asked Clover. 'Did you forget something?'

'No,' said Wilf. And, briefly, he summarised Grampy's strange tale.

'. . . and it was when he said about the red shoes,' he finished. 'The phantom horse was odd enough, but when he said about the shoes, I don't know why, it sort of rang warning bells in my head. And then, when he mentioned a floating cake, it all kind of pointed to some sort of major weirdness going on and I guessed you were in trouble.'

'Thanks, anyway,' said Clover.

'Ah, forget it. The thing is, what do we do now?'

The two of them peered through the trees at the dark cottage.

'We've got to get back in,' said Clover. 'It could

take off at any time. I'm not having her fly off with all my things. Everything I own is in there. And we've got to rescue Neville.'

'Oh,' said Wilf. 'He's in there, is he? Where?'

'I don't know. He ran upstairs to hide. He's really scared. I've never seen him in such a funk. Mrs Eckles told me she was really mean to him when he was a kitten.'

'So what do you suggest?'

'The cherry tree,' said Clover, after a moment's thought. 'One of its branches nearly touches my window. We'll have to sneak around the side to the back, then climb up the tree, wriggle across, and get in that way.'

'You must be joking! We'll break our necks. I'm hopeless at climbing.'

'I'm not, though. You can wait below. I'll get my stuff and throw everything down to you. Then I'll look for Neville.'

'No way. You're not going in that cottage by yourself.'

'Yes I am, there's no choice. Come on, we're wasting time. And whatever happens, don't trip over the log pile.'

A short time later, they stood beneath the cherry

tree in the back garden. All was quiet in the cottage. The back door was firmly closed. No chink in the curtains. No clue as to what might be going on inside.

Clover peered up into the branches, choosing the grips she would use and noting which limbs would take her weight and which wouldn't. She examined the projecting branch that stretched almost to her window. Almost, but not quite.

'All right,' she whispered. 'I'm ready. Give me a bunk-up.'

Wilf made a stirrup with his hands. She put her foot in it, and he boosted her up on to the thickest lower branch.

'Be careful,' whispered Wilf. And Clover began to climb.

She was indeed good at climbing. When she was little, Pa used to take her to work with him sometimes. Clover would swarm up a tree like a monkey and sit watching him, admiring the way his axe flashed in the sun. She hadn't done it for a long time, of course. Pa hadn't worked for ages. Besides, tree climbing was for babies, not respectable girls of nearly eleven.

But she still remembered how to do it.

Quickly, steadily, she moved on up. Down below,

Wilf watched her anxiously. The branches were getting thinner the higher she climbed.

'Careful,' he called again, in a low undertone. 'Slow down.'

'Sssh!' Clover glanced down and put a finger to her lips. She had reached the long limb that jutted out towards the window. She took a steadying breath, lowered herself on to the branch, gripped it with her knees, pushed herself away from the trunk and began sliding out.

Wilf watched her inch her way along, heart in his mouth. The branch was swaying alarmingly. Small twigs and pink blossom floated down on to his head. A leaf landed on his nose, and he fought the urge to sneeze.

Clover had nearly reached the end of the branch. It was bending so low that she was now beneath the window sill. There was still quite a gap between her and the ivy-covered wall. Hardly able to watch, Wilf saw her push herself up into a sitting position. Slowly, carefully, she leaned forward, her right arm outstretched towards the ivy. The branch dipped lower. She leaned out even further.

Wilf closed his eyes. There was a swishing noise above. He waited for the cry and the thump. Which never came.

When he dared open them again, the branch had sprung back into its original position. To his intense relief, Clover was leaning out of the window, waving down at him. Then she turned and was gone.

Wilf bit his lip. He had never been good with heights. He preferred to stay firmly on the ground, which is why he spent his life delivering boxes. What should he do? Wait below and let a girl take all the risks, like a great sissy? It was hardly heroic. On the other hand, if he tried climbing up after her, he wouldn't make it. He would come crashing down, probably break every bone in his body and bring Mesmeranza rushing out of the cottage. Or even worse, freeze! Get halfway along the branch, and just cling there, unable to go back or forward.

It was then that he heard the noise.

It was a strange, deep, rumbling noise, and it came from the cottage. It seemed to emanate from low down. It sounded like stones grinding together. Roots being torn apart. Foundations crumbling. To his horror, he could see the walls shaking!

As he watched, a section of guttering came loose and swung to and fro from a rusting bolt. A piece of thatch detached itself and fell into the herb bed with a thud. Ivy leaves fluttered down, and from somewhere high above, a brick came loose and dropped on to the roof of the chicken coop, sending Flo and Doris into a fit of hysterical squawking.

And then he saw something else. Small, dark shapes, moving towards him across the lawn. There were dozens – no, *scores* of them. Hundreds, maybe! They were making a panicky, chittering noise.

Mice!

More blossom was raining down from the cherry tree. He stretched out his hand and touched the trunk. It was vibrating! He could feel it through his fingers, up his arms, even in his teeth. Below his feet, the ground was quivering. And from all around came that terrible rumbling!

He looked up. Clover was back at the window. He could see her pale, shocked face staring down at him.

There was only one thing to do. He took a flying leap at the lowest branch, grasped it, swung one knee over and somehow heaved himself up on to his stomach. Then, desperately, he began to climb.

Wilf's climbing technique was very different to Clover's. He didn't test branches to see if they would bear his weight. He didn't look for the obvious route. He scrabbled. He slithered. He grabbed, missed, and grabbed again, grazing his palms, skinning his knees, bashing his head and gathering fistfuls of splinters at every turn.

The rumbling noise was getting even louder. It was as though the cottage was at the centre of its very own earthquake. Down below, thin cracks were running across the lawn. Wildly, Wilf fought his way up higher. The tree was trembling horribly. He had nearly reached the long branch now. Clover was at the window, shaking her head, making desperate flapping motions with her hands.

'Don't do it!' she was shouting. 'Go back, you'll fall, it's too late!'

Wilf lowered himself on to his stomach, forced his eyes away from the sickening drop and dragged himself forward. The branch was vibrating so violently that it was all he could do to hold on. He gritted his teeth and wriggled ever onwards.

The window was closer now. Closer . . . closer . . . nearly there . . .

Crack! The sound came from behind. At the same time, the branch jerked downwards.

It was splitting!

And at exactly that moment, an even more night-marish thing happened.

The cottage began to rise! Slowly, with terrible grinding, ripping, rending sounds, it wrenched itself from

the ground – and elevated. Not too high, because the creepers that clung to the walls were holding it down, like mooring ropes on a hot air balloon. But they wouldn't last long. Already, the flimsier ones were beginning to snap under the strain.

'Jump!' screamed Clover. 'Quick, Wilf! Jump!'

Wilf jumped. There was nothing else he could do if he wasn't to be left behind. That was unthinkable. He let out a despairing howl, kicked with his feet, closed his eyes and blindly launched himself into thin air. The tips of his flailing fingertips brushed the window sill – and missed! Then, miraculously, his clawing hands closed on the main stem of the ivy. The rest of his body slammed into the wall, knocking the breath from his lungs. For a moment, he hung there, arms cracking, feet swinging over empty space. The toe of his right boot found a tiny ledge. It was a very tiny ledge. So tiny, that already his boot was beginning to slip . . .

A hand grasped the back of his jacket.

'I've got you,' said Clover's voice, from just above. 'Stay calm and give me your right hand.'

'Can't,' croaked Wilf. His cheek lay against rough stone and the ivy was scratching his face. The wall was vibrating crazily. 'Daren't let go!'

'You've got to! I'm counting to three, and you'll

give me your hand and heave yourself up with the other one. One –'

'I can't!'

'Two –'

'I can't!'

'Three!'

Chapter Twenty

The Flight

'All right?' asked Clover, over her shoulder. Her voice was muffled, because she was leaning precariously out over the window sill, staring down in horrified wonder.

Below, the garden was in tumult. More cracks were appearing, leaves and blossom were flying around wildly and the creepers attached to the cottage walls were slowly being dragged from the earth. Roots were emerging, with clumps of soil sticking to them. Flo and Doris were crouched on their upturned chicken coop, making panicked chicken noises.

'Never better,' groaned Wilf. He lay on his stomach on the floor, hair matted with twigs, leaves, blossom and general filth. His shoulder was in agony, from where he had banged it on the window sill. His shirt was ripped. His hands were pricked by a thousand tiny splinters.

The floor was trembling violently, along with everything else in the room. All around them, there were creaks and groans as the straining cottage fought to become airborne.

There was a ripping noise from down below in the garden, followed by a loud twang as a large section of creeper broke away. The room gave a sudden lurch, and wobbled violently. One end tilted down, and the floor suddenly became a hill. Clover clung to the window sill to stop herself sliding down the slope. Wilf, however, had nothing to hang on to.

Helplessly, he went rolling down the slope, cracking his head on the leg of the bed in passing and ending up in a crumpled heap against the far wall. Clover's table fell over with a crash, shedding all her things, including the jug and wash basin. The basin rolled off into a far corner and the jug smashed into pieces.

The room was in uproar. Everything was rolling and sliding and slithering and falling off hooks as the floor banked even more steeply. Clover was at the top, clinging on to the window sill while her boots scrabbled for purchase on the sloping floor boards.

Then there was a terrible lurch, and the floor tilted back again – only to start tipping the other way! Everything began sliding in the opposite direction. Wilf found himself rising. And there was still nothing to hold on to! He could feel himself beginning to slide . . .

Then there was another lurch. Once again, before he could really take it in, Wilf was at the bottom and Clover was again at the top. It was like being stuck on a horrible see-saw.

The hill was becoming really steep now. To Wilf's horror, Clover's heavy chest of drawers began sliding towards him, like a toboggan hurtling down a snowy slope. He threw himself to one side. It missed him by a whisker, collided with the wall and fell on its side. All the drawers shot out, depositing Clover's precious belongings on the floor.

There was another almighty jerk. Ancient timbers screamed in protest as the floor rocked violently, like a ship in a hurricane. From somewhere down below came distant tinkling and crashing noises.

Then – with a loud twanging noise – the last restraining creeper broke.

'Aaaaaah!' screamed Clover. 'Hold on, we're going uuuuuuup . . .'

Wilf threw his arms over his head and curled into a tight ball. He felt a strange, sinking sensation, as though his stomach was being left behind while the rest of him was rising. That was a shame, as it contained the last of his breakfast.

Then – all of sudden – the whole horrible process just – stopped. The floor levelled out. The creaking noises subsided. The walls ceased to shudder. All the things scattered around the floor gradually rolled to a halt.

Everything went very, very quiet. Quiet and still. The only thing that moved was the curtain hanging to one side of the window. It gently flapped in the cold night breeze.

Slowly, Clover pulled herself up – and looked out.

What she saw was heart-stopping.

They were flying! Flying swiftly and smoothly through the star-spangled sky. Overheard, a full moon shone, casting silver light on the land below. There was no sign of the garden. Already, that had been left far behind. Instead, they were sailing over treetops. Dark, never-ending treetops.

'Oh my!' she breathed. 'Wilf – come and look at this.'

'Get back!' croaked Wilf. 'Move away from there!'

'Don't be silly, it's stopped rocking. You can stand up now.'

Wilf dragged himself to his feet. Arms extended for balance, he stepped gingerly out into the room. Walking with a nervous, bow-legged gait, alert for any unexpected dips or wobbles, he lurched across to join her. Fearfully, he peered over her shoulder, looked out . . .

And down.

His stomach flipped. He clapped his hand to his mouth and stepped smartly to one side, pressing his back against the wall and closing his eyes.

'Look!' Clover pointed down, excitedly. 'We're over Tingly Bottom! I can see the lights in the tavern! I bet Pa's in there!'

'That's nice,' said Wilf faintly.

'There's the river. It looks really small from up here. Look!'

'I won't just now, if you don't mind.'

'But you're missing it all.'

'No, no. I'm just taking it easy. You tell me all

about it, I'm listening.'

'But it's wonderful! Everything's so tiny! We're going even higher. Open your eyes and look!'

'Just leave me alone for a moment, would you? I'm trying to think about low things. Mushrooms. Moles . . .'

There came the sudden, violent crash of a trapdoor.

'Well, well. Unexpected visitors!'

A sharp new voice broke into Wilf's thoughts.

Unwillingly, he opened his eyes. A woman's head was sticking up through the hole. A woman's head he – knew? Or did he? There was something about the white face, the red lips and the hard green eyes, which right now were fixed on Clover. He felt certain he had seen this head before – but when? Where?

'What a stubborn girl you are, Clover Twig,' said the head. 'I thought I'd got rid of you, but it seems you're determined to come along for the ride. And I see you have young Master Wilfred I-Don't-Like-Tomatoes Brownswoody with you. Friends, are you? How touching.'

She turned her green gaze on Wilf – and instantly, his brain cleared. It was as though a fog lifted. Of course he remembered her. The strange woman in the forest! The one who had gone on and on about cake. The one who had looked at him through funny glasses. It all came flooding back to him. In fact, he suddenly realised he knew her from *before*. She was none other than the old tomato-seller from the previous year! It was only now that he made the connection. Everything made sense, now it was too late to do anything about it.

'You've met?' enquired Clover, with a surprised look at Wilf. 'You never said.'

'I forgot,' admitted Wilf. 'It was the funny glasses. She wiped my brain.'

'He means the Hypnospecs,' said Mesmeranza. 'They worked rather better on him than on you. That's because he was empty-headed to start with.'

Wilf glared and said nothing.

'Not in the mood for talking? Suit yourself. I can't stay here chatting anyway, I have to get back down. No rest for the wicked.'

'That suits us just fine,' said Clover. 'We're choosy about the company we keep.'

'Mind your mouth, miss!' The green eyes narrowed. 'Much more from you and I shall be forced to wield the Wand again. Of course, it's a *very* long way to fall.'

'Don't do that,' said Wilf hastily. 'She didn't mean

it. She's had a long day, haven't you, Clover?'

'Ah well. She'll have plenty of time for sleep when we reach Coldiron. Not a lot else to do when you're rotting in the dungeons.'

'Mrs Eckles will know,' said Clover. 'She'll come after us.'

'Ah, but you see, she can't get in. The castle's a fortress. Protection spells, darling. Big, strong, castle-sized ones. Two can play at that game. I've been working on them for years. Rather amusingly, I used Demelza's own recipe, so her own magic is turned against her. No, I wouldn't rely on her if I were you. I'm shutting you in now, and I shall be taking the ladder away. I suggest you hold on tight when we land. Bernard's a little rusty. Enjoy the trip!'

And with that the trapdoor closed, with a crash.

Down in the kitchen, the rocking chair was lying on its side. The table had slid halfway across the room. The saucepan full of milk had toppled off the stove and lay in a white puddle. Various items were scattered on the floor, including the cake, which lay in a pile of crumbs. To add to the effect, the scene was lit by eerie green light.

The private cupboard was wide open. The severed

padlock chain lay on the floor. It was still smoking a bit.

'Children. They are *so* annoying,' announced Mesmeranza from the doorway. 'They're almost as irritating as you Imps. They're always on the side of *good*, do you notice?'

'Imps don't take sides,' said Bernard. 'We're imp-artial. Don't talk, I'm concentrating.'

He was sitting cross-legged on the middle shelf. Floating in the air, midway between his tiny webbed hands, was the bubble containing the miniature cottage. This time, however, there was no garden. The cottage hung suspended in the very centre, surrounded by blackness. If you looked really carefully, you could see tiny pinpricks of light whizzing around.

'I thought you knew how to do this,' said Mesmeranza. She perched on the edge of the kitchen table, reached into her handbag, took out a compact and proceeded to powder her nose.

'I *do* know,' snapped Bernard. 'I just haven't done it for a while, that's all. Stop needling me when I'm working.'

'You've always got an excuse, haven't you? Even when we were children. It's never *your* fault. Always a rubbish take-off. Every single time. Everything falling about everywhere. Just look at the cake, it's in pieces.'

'Well, I'm very sorry about the *cake*,' said Bernard tightly. 'I'm very sorry that a highly complicated procedure like getting a large cottage airborne resulted in a spoiled *cake*.'

'I suppose you'll make a mess of the landing too. You always do.'

'*I do not*.'

'You do. You've never been any good. Trust us to get a flying cottage with an inferior Imp.'

'Look, do you *mind*? I'm trying to keep us steady. It's not as easy as it looks.'

'Nonsense. You're rubbish at it, that's all. Just don't get us lost, that's all I ask. How are we doing? Much further?'

'We'd get there a lot sooner if you'd just let me get on with the job.'

Bernard made a tiny adjustment with his left hand. The kitchen floor dipped a little.

'Watch it, fool Imp! I'm trying to put on lipstick here!'

'That's right,' snapped Bernard. 'You see to the important stuff. Just let me fly the cottage, that's all right.'

Mesmeranza gave an impatient sigh, hopped off

the table and strode over to the kitchen window. She jerked back the curtain and peered out. The night was filled with streaming stars. The silver moon was keeping pace.

'Up, up and away,' she purred. 'Just like the old times. Except that Demelza isn't here to argue about where we're going and spoil everything. I always wanted volcanoes, remember? Burnt-out, blasted landscapes, that was my kind of thing. She always wanted the soppy seaside. Incidentally, we're going the wrong way.'

'What?'

'You took a wrong turn. You should have turned left awhile back, by the big lake, where the forest began thinning out. You went right. I don't know why, you've done it enough times.'

'It's because you keep *talking* . . .'

'Turn round.'

'All right, all right . . .'

'I just knew you'd go wrong. Hurry up, I want to be there by morning.'

'Stop *talking* . . .'

'Do an emergency stop. One moment, I need to hold on to something. All right, *now*!'

Bernard moved his small webbed green hands in a complicated, anti-clockwise motion, ending with a sharp clap. The cottage came to a sudden, abrupt halt. Everything went scooting across the room. From somewhere upstairs came the sound of faint screams and bodies rolling.

'Hear that?' said Mesmeranza. 'Frightened children having a hard time. Music to my ears.'

Chapter Twenty-One

The Cottage Arrives

'Boss? Wake up! We're in business!'
  'Wha'?'

Humperdump Chunk opened his eyes blearily. He had been dreaming about marrying Miss Fly. All her cats were pageboys and bridesmaids, decked out with little flowery bonnets and ribbons tied to their tails. The blushing bride wore a veil of stitched-together hankies. They were about to tuck into the wedding feast, which consisted mainly of fish heads. It was a happy dream and he didn't want to wake up.

'You're wanted upstairs, boss. She's done it.'

'Wha'? Who?'

'Her ladyship! She's got the cottage!'

'Eh?'

'The cottage. The one she's always on about. It's arrived. Just flown in. I can't believe you didn't hear the bump. It's parked out in the courtyard. There's prisoners.'

'Prisoners?'

'Yep. Come on, she's waitin'.'

Groaning, Humperdump heaved himself up off the old mattress which, despite Mesmeranza's orders, he hadn't yet disposed of. It was an old friend and very heavy to move.

Prisoners. He could have done without this. Prisoners meant he would have to *do* something. They would need to be fed and watered. There would be paperwork. He wouldn't be able to spend so much time courting Miss Fly. They would distract him from the path of true love, which right now wasn't running at all smoothly.

'I'll open the cells, shall I?' asked Jimbo excitedly. 'The ones opposite the door so we can keep an eye on 'em if they gets frisky.'

'Yer,' said Humperdump, reaching for his nail-studded truncheon, which hung from a hook on the wall. 'All right then, Jimbo, you do that.'

'This is more like it, eh, boss? Things is lookin' up. Never thought I'd see the day when she got the flyin' cottage. I still can't believe you didn't hear the bump. Whole place shook. Hurry up, you know what she's like when she's kept waitin'.'

'I know,' sighed Humperdump, and hurried up.

Miss Fly didn't hear the bump either. She too was fast asleep. She had been up all night sneezing and had only just dozed off. She was alerted by the cats, who all tried to jump into bed with her at the same time. She gave a little shriek, sneezed, groped for her hankie on the bedside table and stared around in the dim early morning light. More bits of plaster had fallen from the ceiling during the night, but she didn't think that was what was causing the panic.

'Jusd a biddit, darligs, jusd a biddit,' cried Miss Fly.

She struggled out of bed, dislodged a kitten from her hairy nightgown, brushed the tortoiseshell from her shoulder and thrust her feet into a pair of hairy slippers. Picking a careful path through the empty plates and brimming litter trays, she waded to the window in a squalling sea of fur and peered down into the courtyard.

Which had a cottage sitting in it.

Unsurprisingly, it was causing quite a stir. As Miss Fly watched, the captain of the guard came running from an archway, pulling on his plumed helmet and tripping over his sword. He was followed by his troops, all three of them in various stages of undress. Mrs Chunk had hurried from the kitchens and was standing in a doorway, mouth open, a rolling pin in her hand. Maidservants, footmen and boot-boys were gathered in little clumps, staring and pointing.

The back of the cottage – what used to be the pretty side – directly faced Miss Fly's window. Standing in the doorway, face ablaze with triumph, was Mesmeranza. On either side of her stood two dishevelled, grim-faced children.

'Fly?' shouted Mesmeranza. 'What d'you think you're doing? Get down here immediately, and bring your notebook!'

Miss Fly scurried for her dressing gown.

Down below, Mesmeranza turned to the children.

'Well,' she said. 'Here we all are. Castle Coldiron. First impressions anybody?'

Clover and Wilf said nothing. There was nothing

to say. Besides, they were both in a state of shock. The soles of their feet still tingled from the impact of the touchdown, which had been truly horrible, involving tall spires suddenly rising outside the windows, followed by a massive bump as all the windows simultaneously shattered, sprinkling the floor with shards of glass.

And then, at wandpoint, they had reluctantly stepped from the cottage . . . and into another world. A cold, grey world of towering stone walls and curious, staring faces.

The captain of the guard came hurrying up, trying to pull on his gloves and salute at the same time. His helmet plume waved in the cold breeze.

'Place a guard on the cottage, Captain,' ordered Mesmeranza. 'Nobody is to enter but me. Ah. Here comes Chunk.'

The crowds parted as a gigantic man came lumbering through, holding a large bunch of keys and a big studded truncheon.

Over by the kitchen door, Mrs Chunk gave a proud smile and announced, 'That's my boy.'

'This is Master Chunk,' said Mesmeranza. 'He'll be giving you a guided tour of the dungeons. I'm sure you'll become great friends over the next few years.'

'What about the cottage?' asked Clover. She glanced back over her shoulder.

The cottage wasn't staring now. It just looked – tired. Old, tired and more than ready for retirement. The flight hadn't done it any favours. Almost all the thatch had blown away. More bits had dropped off, including the chimney. All the windows were broken. Wind-torn ivy drooped from the walls.

'What about it?'

'What will you do with it? Now you've got your own way and it's finally yours?'

'I shall get rid of it,' said Mesmeranza dismissively. 'I shall leave it parked here for a day or two and enjoy the sweet smell of success. I'll have my picture painted, standing in the doorway holding a large sign saying MINE NOW. I shall send the picture to Demelza, with a first-class stamp. And then I shall demolish it.'

'So you won't even *use* it?' asked Wilf. 'You went to all that trouble for something you're just going to *destroy*?'

'You just don't get it, do you? I don't *want* it. I mean, just look at it, it's a wreck. I just don't want Demelza to have it. Ah, here comes Fly. You took your time.'

Miss Fly came running up clutching a little black

book and wearing an old brown dressing gown which was plastered in cat hairs.

'Sorry,' she wheezed. 'Cabe as quig as I could.'

'I hope you've put the champagne on ice. That's Number One on the new list. Celebrate With Champagne. Number Two is Have Picture Painted And Post It To Demelza. Although –' Mesmeranza gave a little titter, 'although I'm not sure where to send it, now she's homeless. *The Cottage-shaped hole in the ground.* That should get there, don't you think?'

'Mrs Eckles was right,' said Clover disgustedly. 'You really *are* spiteful.'

'Take them down to the dungeons, Chunk,' ordered Mesmeranza. 'Separate cells, bread and water only. We'll see if hunger will make them less insolent.'

A heavy hand descended on to Clover's shoulder. At the same time, Wilf felt something hard and spiky dig into the base of his spine. The gigantic man said in a rather comically high voice, 'Get walking.'

There was nothing to do but get walking.

Back in the cupboard, Bernard was putting his bubble back in the sack. If he felt a twinge of conscience, he certainly wasn't showing it. So what if the kids were captured? None of his concern. Anyway, he'd done the job. Back home he had lasagne in the oven.

He vanished, just like that.

Chapter Twenty-Two

Captured in the Castle

At this point we must leave Clover and Wilf to shuffle off to their fate. Unlike Bernard, we must stay with the cottage.

It didn't take long for it to lose its novelty. The dramatic manner of its arrival had initially caused great excitement. The crowd had hung around for a bit, hoping the cottage might do something else –

but it hadn't. The arrest of the two prisoners had been interesting, but they were gone now. So was Mesmeranza, who had swept away with Miss Fly scurrying at her heels. Then it began drizzling, so people had drifted away.

The cottage sat in a mess of broken glass, right in the middle of the courtyard, which was clearly going to be a real nuisance. People would have to skirt round it. They were already grumbling that it was an eyesore and wondering how long it would remain there cluttering up the place.

A solitary sentry stood on guard in the doorway. His name was Stan and he didn't want to be there. It was boring. He hoped his shift would end soon. He couldn't see the point of standing in the rain guarding an empty cottage. All right, so it had flown in. There were no signs that it was about to fly out again, so why bother?

Up in the attic room, everything was still. Clover's chest of drawers still lay on its side and the bed stuck out into the room at an angle. The window hung from one hinge. All the glass was missing and only the frame remained, ensnared in the tendrils of ivy. A gust of wind blew in, bringing rain.

Then something moved. A lump under the blanket on the bed. A moving lump. A lump which slowly travelled up towards the pillow end. There was a scrabbling noise and finally a head emerged. A black, furry head, with two ears – one nibbled – and two yellow eyes.

Neville.

He wriggled out on to the pillow, dug his claws in, and s-t-r-e-t-c-h-ed. He sat up. Then he began washing himself. He did his paws, his tail and his whiskers and left the rest. It was a bit of a lick and a promise, because Neville lived in a forest. His coat was so matted and full of random vegetation that he never really got to the root of things and the smell was always there. But he always washed first. It was the Cat Way. Wash first. Then Eat. Then Snooze, while the food went down.

There were other things he sometimes did, of course. Favourites included: Play With Something Small And Squeaky, Rather Nastily, In Corner; Rampage Around Forest Driving Off Wolves And Fighting Foxes; Return To Hero's Welcome And Big Fuss. In between all this was a lot of sitting around, staring at nothing. All cats do this. No one knows why.

Ablutions over, Neville thumped down off the bed and stared around.

Things seemed – different, somehow. The furniture

was all wrong and there was stuff all over the floor. Something about the window had changed. Oh, *riiii-iight*. It wasn't there any more, that was it.

Neville felt vaguely surprised.

You should know a bit more about Neville. Despite Mrs Eckles' claim that he is intelligent and can Understand Everything You Say, he isn't and he can't. All right, so he's a witch cat and has lived a lot more lives than the usual nine. But he's still just a cat. His brain only stores so much. He has very little in the way of long-term memory. Even when he does remember things, he can't make much sense of them. So he sticks with the basics – food, sleep, warmth and hunting. Everything else is a mystery.

Neville looked about him in mild puzzlement. For the life of him he couldn't remember what he was doing in Clover's bed. Had something bad happened?

He dimly recalled that there had been some kind of drama the night before, sending him scurrying for cover under the blankets, fur on end and heart pounding. It must have been some fright. He had clearly been in a panic, because there were great big rips in the bottom sheet. And then, exhausted by it all, whatever it was, he must have gone to sleep, because now it was clearly morning.

What should he do?

Eat, that's what. He would find Mistress and remind her about breakfast.

Oh, but wait. Hadn't Mistress gone off somewhere?

Neville had a blurry recollection of a lot of kissing and her riding off in a donkey cart. Why had she gone? He didn't know. Where had she gone? He hadn't a clue. When had she gone? He wasn't sure. What had happened after she had gone? He couldn't remember.

Something was definitely *wrong*. Where were the usual sounds? He couldn't hear the birds singing, or the swish of the cherry tree, or the clink of his milk bowl being set ready for breakfast.

Neville padded across to the window, placed his paws on the sill and looked out. His yellow eyes widened, and his whole body went stiff.

The garden was gone. The cherry tree was gone. The chickens were gone. The forest was gone. All around rose high walls. He was looking down at a deserted, rainswept courtyard.

Neville dropped back to the floor and sat thinking. Well, not exactly thinking. It was more a state of vague bewilderment. Did he know this place? Had this sort of thing happened before? If so, was he always this surprised?

Of course, the answers to these questions were yes, yes and yes. Ever since he was a kitten, Neville had lived in a flying cottage. He was old now. Over the years, there had been many occasions involving weird green light in the kitchen and a small green talking thing in the private cupboard and stars streaming past the windows. Numerous times when the forest had disappeared and the world outside had changed, offering unsettling new sights, new smells and interesting new fighting opportunities.

But Neville remembered none of them. Each time was as though it had never happened before. Because he was just a cat, he was never prepared and always confused. Life was a mystery and that was that. In the meantime, he would go and check the food bowl.

Neville rose to his feet and was just about to pad across to the trap door, when he was distracted. This happens a lot with cats. They set out with a definite purpose, then get sidelined into doing something completely different.

All kinds of tempting things lay strewn across the floor: a comb, bits of broken glass, a pincushion. Neville was overtaken by a skittish urge to *play* with something. Not his boring old downstairs toys.

Something new. A whole new world of playful opportunity lay before him. He would investigate.

He sniffed at the comb. He eyed the pincushion. He considered the glass. All of them looked a bit sharp, a bit awkward, a bit pointy. Then something caught his eye. Something in the dark regions under the bed. The perfect size, the perfect shape. Something that was just dying to be batted about.

It was a glass bottle.

Neville liked the look of the bottle. He just knew what would happen if he dabbed at it with his paw. It would *slide*. Oh, what fun! It would slide and slither, that bottle, and he would follow it and dab at it again. Maybe flip it in the air. Stalk it. Whack it about a bit.

He went into a hunting crouch, rear end wriggling. He'd get that bottle! He'd leap on it unawares, he would, and send it for six!

Slowly, keeping low, he crept forward, towards the bed.

He pounced!

His front paw swiped at the bottle and it slid, just like he knew it would. Neville ran after it, caught up with it and scooped it into the air. It banged on the underside of the bed, then went slithering across the floor. Neville charged after it and caught it under his paw.

Oh. Wait a minute. This wasn't good.

Neville lifted his paw and inspected it. It was all wet. The stopper had come off and the bottle was leaking. Perhaps it wasn't so good to play with after all.

He raised the damp paw to his nose. Funny smell. He gave an experimental lick. It didn't taste exactly *good*, but Neville was a cat and had stepped in much worse things.

He licked again. And again.

And then . . .

And *then* . . .

REVELATION!

'Excuse me?' shouted Wilf. He banged on the bars of his cell. The sound echoed along the stone corridor. 'Hey! A bit of service here!'

'What?' snapped Humperdump Chunk. He was sitting in the guardroom across the way, laboriously filling out a form with a stubby pencil.

'Will the food be arriving soon? We're hungry.'

'Jimbo's gettin' it. I'm fillin' out the paperwork.'

'What are you writing?' asked Clover. 'Is it about us?'

She was in the cell next door to Wilf's. Both of them stood at the bars, staring out. There was a thick

stone wall between them, so they couldn't see each other, but at least they could talk. That was something.

'Yer. I gotta write down the date. And the time o' your arrival. An' yer full names.'

'Ah, but you don't know what they are, do you?'

'No.' Humperdump scratched behind his ear. 'What are they?'

'Hortensia Splodgepudding,' announced Clover promptly.

'King Bobby Gobby the Third,' said Wilf.

They both sniggered a bit. It was a refreshing sound in this damp, shadowy, horrible place.

'Think that's funny, do you?' said Humperdump. 'Think that's a big laugh? You won't be laughin' soon.'

He kicked out a heavily booted foot and the guardroom door crashed shut, hiding him from view.

'Clover?' whispered Wilf.

'What?'

'Are you all right?'

'Fine, thank you.'

'We've got to get out of here. The gaoler's stupid, that's something. Maybe we can trick him. Put a sleeping potion in his food or something.'

'Great idea. Let's send out for some.'

254

'You don't have a nail file in your pocket, by any chance? Or something sharp?'

'What, so you can saw through the bars?'

'No. So I can pick out some of these splinters.'

'Oh,' said Clover. 'No, sorry.'

There was a little silence.

'I don't suppose you can bend the bars at all, can you?' suggested Clover not very hopefully. 'With your strong delivery boy arms?'

'Sadly, no. Hey! You don't happen to handily have the Changeme Serum, by any chance?'

'No. I put it in the chest. It probably got smashed, along with everything else.'

'That's a shame. We might have done something with that. You could have taken it this time and gone on a rampage and kicked the door down. What are you doing in there? I can hear you rustling about.'

'Tidying up the straw.'

Wilf relaxed a bit. She was tidying. That was a good sign. A great pity about the serum, though. A rampage might have come in useful.

Chapter Twenty-Three

Neville Goes Walkies

Something wonderful had happened to Neville. The moment he had licked the Changeme Serum from his paw, there had a been a big, lightning flash of illumination. It was like a thousand pieces of randomly scattered jigsaw puzzle all rising up and fitting themselves together, making a perfect picture. In short, he had gone all clever.

His brain was now a keen-edged sword. It cut away all the stupid cat-based rubbish and went right to the heart of things. For once, in all his nine lives, he had a proper grasp of what was going on.

He knew the answers to all the questions that had been bothering him. Where was he? In Castle Coldiron. How had he got there? The cottage had been stolen. Who by? Mesmeranza, Mistress's horrible sister, who used to dangle him over wells. Why? Because she was like that. Oh this incredible joined-up thinking! It was like being born anew. Of course, on a practical level things weren't looking good. It was clearly up to him to sort things out. The children were gone for a start. Probably taken prisoner. He would have to investigate the dungeons. Find a way of rescuing them. Maybe some sort of cunning diversion.

Neville considered his plan of campaign. He needed to find the children, outwit the witch and make sure the cottage got back to the forest, hopefully before Mistress arrived home, found it gone and got all worried. Fiendishly complicated – but not to a cat with a shiny new brain.

First, he would find out the lie of the land. He would have to make his way into the castle. That should be easy; he knew the place like the back of his paw because, of course, he used to live there. Once in, he would slink, spy, and – *listen*.

Now, there was a thought! He would finally be able to make sense of human speech, which up to now had always been a sort of background drone. *Blah-blah-blah-blah-Neville-blah-blah-blah-dinner-blah-blah*. That's what it had sounded like. But not any more. He would be able to understand human conversations! Even join in, give the cat's point of view! How great would *that* be!

Neville decided to experiment. He would try saying something. He would try saying his own name.

'Nnmmm . . .' tried Neville. 'Nnmmmiiiaaaow.'

Not promising. He would attempt something else. He would try saying *milk*.

'Mmmm . . .' tried Neville. 'Mmmmmmiiiaaaaow.'

Nope. No good. Everything turned into *miaow*. His throat and mouth just weren't the right shape to produce actual words.

But, hey! So what? He still had the brain, didn't he? He could still listen. He was now that unique thing – a cat who really *could* Understand Everything You Said. And mentally dismiss it as a load of rubbish, because he was so, *so* much cleverer than you.

So. He would go downstairs, slip quietly out of a

window, stealthily make his way into the castle and do whatever needed to be done. But first, he would make a quick little detour to the stables. There was somebody there he very much wanted to see.

Booboo the flying horse stood in his stable, munching a mouthful of hay. His Special Vanishing Saddle was off, so he was currently very definitely *there*.

Up to now, we have only heard about Booboo. He flies. Sometimes he is invisible. He can make his own way home. He has an evil disposition. That's about it, really.

Let's have a proper look at him. He is big, jet black and muscular. He has all the normal horse things – long face, rolling eyes, twitchy ears, swishy tail and four legs. But being a flying horse, he also boasts two large feathery wings. They grow out of his shoulders and, when extended, take up a lot of room. He only uses them when airborne. On the ground they're just a nuisance, so most of the time, he keeps them folded away.

Booboo's evil disposition makes him a hard horse to ride. Full gallop followed by emergency stop, that's his style. As a sideline, he offers a full range of horrible horse habits: bucking, rearing, kicking, shying, nipping and walking too close to walls.

He has other weird little ways. He doesn't like the colour purple and refuses to fly over plum trees or fields of lavender. He dislikes loud noises, scarecrows and cats. He is petrified of small, scuttling things – particularly mice. Booboo's biggest nightmare would be a cat up a plum tree with a mouse in its jaws and a scarecrow standing by playing a trumpet. So far this has never happened.

Booboo swallowed his hay and helped himself to another mouthful. He liked being in his stable. It was warm and dry and there was plenty to eat. There had been some sort of disturbance in the courtyard earlier. A loud bump, which had made the ground shake. Whatever it was, it was enough to make the groom go running off to have a look. He hadn't returned, so Booboo was all alone. Hay, peace and quiet. Everything was well in Flying Horse World. Until he saw the cat.

He knew that cat.

Booboo disliked all cats, but he particularly hated *this* cat. He had had dealings with this cat long ago in the distant past. Booboo clearly remembered kicking it once, very hard, when it was little more than a kitten. It had come running merrily into the stable and started jumping around his back legs. So Booboo had kicked it, sending it hurtling through the air into a pile of something you find in stables that is very nasty indeed.

The cat was older now, of course. Older, bigger and a darned sight more ugly. Booboo hadn't seen it for a long, long time and had thought it was gone for ever. And now it had come back to haunt him.

The cat was sitting in the doorway, carefully observing him. There was something about the unblinking yellow gaze that Booboo didn't like. Something *knowing*.

Uneasily, Booboo eyed the cat.

The cat stared.

Booboo showed the whites of his eyes and tossed his mane.

The cat still stared.

Boo pawed the ground with his front hoof.

More staring from the cat.

Booboo gave a warning whinny and rustled his furled wings.

Slowly, the cat stood up. The eyes still stared, but the mouth – well, the mouth almost seemed to be *grinning*. For the first time, Booboo noticed that there was something trapped under its right paw. Something small and wiggly. Was it? Could it be . . .?

Arrrgh! A mouse!

Everything happened very fast. There was a flash

of fur, and suddenly the cat was on top of the rail that ran around Booboo's stall. The mouse was dangling upside down from its mouth on the end of a long, thin tail.

The cat opened its jaws. Deliberately, accurately, and with a great sense of purpose, it dropped the mouse into Booboo's manger, where it began running around under the hay letting out a series of small, surprised squeaks.

The cat watched Booboo's reaction for a long moment. There was a lot of reaction to watch. Panicked whinnying, mad eye-rolling, rearing, crashing, splintered wood flying through the air. It was all there.

When the cat had seen enough, it dusted off its two front paws, jumped down and strolled out of the stable, smirking.

Jimbo Squint came down the long stone passage, carrying a tray. On it were two tin plates, each containing a small crust of stale bread, together with two mugs of water.

He came to a halt outside the cell containing Wilf, who was slumped against the bars, despondently picking splinters from his hands.

'Stand back,' ordered Jimbo. 'Right back, against

the wall. I'm pushin' yer food under the door.'

'What is it?' asked Wilf hopefully. He hadn't eaten a thing since the sugar lumps of the day before and he was ravenous.

'Bread and water, like she ordered.'

'Yummy,' said Wilf. 'Hear that, Clover? I hope you're hungry! We've got bread and water!'

'What, no cake?'

'I'll ask. My friend's just wondering if there's any cake?'

'Preferably one with a file in, please,' called Clover.

'She'd like one with a file in,' Wilf told Jimbo. 'Please. If it's not too much trouble.'

'Well, yer friend can just shut up,' growled Jimbo. 'Any more cheek from either of you and you won't get nothin' at all, so be warned.'

'Is that you, Jimbo?' The door to the guardroom flew open and Humperdump peered out. 'I been waitin' for you.'

'I'm comin', boss. Just feedin' the prisoners.'

'Well, do it quick, then come in 'ere. I needs yer help. And shut the door behind you, I'm sick of hearin' their backchat.'

Humperdump retreated back into the guardroom and sat at his desk. He had given up filling in forms. Jimbo could do it later. Right now, he had something more important on his mind. Before him was a blank sheet of paper. He was about to write the next love note to Miss Fly.

Jimbo entered, closing the door behind him.

'Sit down, Jimbo,' ordered Humperdump. 'I want to get this note writ, and it's gotta be good.'

'I thought you was givin' up on 'er, boss.'

'I'm givin' 'er one last chance. I'm gonna write down that poem o' yours. Let's get crackin'. 'Ow'd it go again?'

'Roses is red . . .'

'Slow down, slow down. Which one's the R again? Is it the straight line with the roundy bit at the top an' the extra little leg . . .?'

Mesmeranza stood at the window of her turret room, sipping green champagne.

'A toast, Fly!' she cried. 'Here's to me finally settling old scores!'

'I haven't got a glass,' said Miss Fly, who was still in her old brown dressing gown. Her allergy wasn't quite so bad this morning. The trip down to the courtyard to view the newly arrived cottage seemed to have cleared her head. Her m's were still missing, but her n's, t's and p's were back in action, which was a relief.

'I'm well aware of that. I'm not going to waste good champagne on you. Not after all your negative remarks and sniffing and eyebrow raising. I expect you're feeling a bit silly now. Are you feeling silly, Fly?'

'I'b feeling *chilly*,' said Miss Fly. 'I'd like to get dressed, if you don't bind.'

'I do mind. I haven't finished with you. I want you to order me a celebration dinner. Something with an apple in its mouth, tell Mrs Chunk. And balloons. The musicians are to compose a song praising me and the footmen are to choreograph and practise a small ballet in my honour. I shall watch it over coffee.'

'Is that all?'

'No. Before the light goes, I shall want you to paint a picture of me posing next to the cottage, looking radiantly youthful.'

'What? But I can't paint!'

'Then learn, quickly.'

'But I haven't got any paints.'

'Then order some. A simple watercolour will do, and it had better be good. I need to choose which gown to wear. I can't decide between red satin and green velvet. I shall consult the Mirror.'

Mesmeranza finished her glass of champagne and

poured herself another one.

'What about the poor little children?' asked Miss Fly.

'What about them?'

'Well, you're not going to keep theb locked up for ever, surely?'

'I don't see why not.'

'But they're *children*. Their fabilies will biss theb.'

'Too bad. They shouldn't have stowed away.'

'But it's not *right*!' cried Miss Fly. 'Putting innocent children down in the dungeons. In the care of that *horrible* ban.'

'Who – Chunk?'

'Yes,' said Miss Fly. 'Hib.'

'I can't help noticing you have a bit of a *thing* about Chunk, Fly. Why is that?'

'I just don't like hib,' mumbled Miss Fly, going pink.

'Any particular reason? Apart from him being fat, incompetent, lazy and stupid?'

'If you *bust* know,' muttered Miss Fly, blushing scarlet, 'he keeps sending be notes.'

'Sending you *notes*? What kind of notes?'

'Love notes,' admitted Miss Fly.

'He does?' Mesmeranza let out a little shriek of laughter. 'Oh, ha ha! Will the wedding be soon, do you think, ha ha ha?'

'It's not funny,' said Miss Fly crossly. 'It's not funny and he's not fit to look after poor little children. It's not *right*.'

'I'll tell you what's not *right*, Fly. What's not *right* is your unhelpful attitude. Or your horrible old dressing gown or your shoes or that posse of stinking mogs you insist on keeping in your room.'

'By cats *do not* stink.'

'They most certainly *do* stink . . .'

And so it went on. Both of them were becoming so heated that they didn't even notice the cat lurking in the shadow of the doorway.

Neville, of course. Neville, the cat genius, listening and learning and taking it all in. So much information. He would use it all.

Chapter Twenty-Four

The Dungeons Again

All was quiet in the castle kitchens. The breakfast rush hour was over, and Mrs Chunk was enjoying a brief ten minutes with her feet up before starting lunch. There were clattering noises from the sinks at the far end, where the maids were finishing the washing up.

She sat at the table with a large mug of tea and a

plate of biscuits. She was just about to sip, when she felt herself being watched.

There was a cat in the doorway. A large black cat with yellow eyes. One of Miss Fly's, of course. It must have got itself locked out of her room and wandered down. Drawn by the smells, she supposed.

'Miaow?' said the cat pleasantly.

'Well now,' said Mrs Chunk. 'What you doin' down 'ere, puss?'

'Miaow,' said the cat. It stalked towards her and rubbed around her ankles.

'Lost, are you? You want some milk?'

Rather to her surprise, the cat – *nodded*. It did it enthusiastically, almost as though it were agreeing with her.

Mrs Chunk reached down and scratched it behind an ear.

'You wait there and I'll get a saucer,' she said. 'Then I'll get one of the maids to take you back up to Miss Fly. How's that?'

She stood up, and immediately the cat jumped into the warm spot where she had been sitting.

'I expect you likes full cream, eh?' said Mrs Chunk.

The cat nodded again. She noticed it looking interestedly at the bucket of fish heads she kept in the corner.

'Fancy a fish head?' enquired Mrs Chunk.

'Miaow,' agreed the cat. To her surprise, it sat back on its hindquarters and held up two paws.

'You want *two*?'

'Miaow miaow.'

Marvelling, Mrs Chunk hurried away to get a saucer. What an unusually clever cat. It was almost as though it could Understand Everything You Said.

Down in the guardroom, Humperdump threw down his pencil and sat back. It had taken some time to get Jimbo's masterpiece committed to paper. He was sweating heavily and had broken two pencils, but it was done.

'That's it!' said Humperdump, surveying his handiwork. '*Roses is red, grey is the sky, cowpats is greeny-brown and I loves Miss Fly*. And I've signed it *Frum Yore Humpy*. An' I done three big crosses fer kisses. If that don't do the trick, I don't know what will.'

'You done a great job, boss,' agreed Jimbo. 'A whole four lines o' poetry an' it only took you a coupla hours to write 'em down.'

'I couldn't 'ave done it without you, Jimbo. All that spellin'. All them good words. I dunno how you thinks of it.'

'Ah, that's what I'm 'ere for. Do all the work an' come up with romantic poems in me spare time.'

'Well, I appreciates it. I just 'ope *she* does.'

''Course she will. I'll take it up right away, shall I? Stick it under 'er door?'

'You do that, Jimbo. Take the master key and nip up through the kitchens, it'll be quicker. And don't mess about this time. Try knockin' an' give it to 'er in person. Wait for a reply, mind. Tell 'er I'm pinin' away an' won't rest till she's mine. And tell Mum I fancies pork chops.'

Outside the guardroom, in the shadowy stone passage, Clover and Wilf stood dejectedly at the bars of their separate cells. There was nothing to do but watch the flickering torches and listen to dripping noises. Time was passing slowly.

'Clover?' whispered Wilf.

'Yes?'

'What are you doing?'

'Nothing. Thinking how to get out of here.'

'Any ideas yet?'

'No.'

There was a short silence.

'Clover?'

'What?'

'Do you think Mrs Eckles will rescue us?'

'I don't see how. You heard Mesmeranza. She can't get past the protection spells.'

There was another silence.

'Clover?'

'Yes?'

'We're in real trouble, aren't we?'

'Yes,' said Clover with a sigh. 'I believe we are.'

She moved back from the bars and sat on the hard bench, staring down at the tin plate. The bread was so stale it had scratched her throat going down. Even the water was brackish, as though it had had things swimming in it.

The guardroom door opened and Jimbo Squint came scuttling out. In one hand he held a large brass key. In the other was a folded piece of paper.

'Push the plates and mugs under the door,' he ordered. 'Then stand back. No sudden moves.'

In silence, Clover and Wilf did as they were told.

'What's this?' jeered Jimbo. 'No backchat? No funny remarks? Finally learnin' a bit of respect, are we? That's good. If yer *very* humble, you might get another crust for yer supper.'

He put the dishes on the tray, then hurried off along the passageway. His footsteps retreated up stone steps.

'I'd like to dong him with his own tray,' said Wilf.

Back up in the kitchens, Neville had consumed two saucers full of milk and was now wolfing down his second fish head. Very tasty it was, too. The perfect combination of crunchy and slimy.

'My,' said Mrs Chunk. 'You *was* a hungry boy, wasn't you? Made a bit of a mess, though.'

He had too. Despite his new brain, Neville still had his usual eating habits. Things tasted so much better when dragged off the plate, kicked around a bit, then eaten off the floor.

His ears pricked at the sudden sound of a key turning in a lock. A door in the far wall crashed open and a small man stepped through, carrying a tray.

''Ere you go, Mrs Chunk,' said Jimbo. 'I brought the tray back up.'

'Ta, Mr Squint. How's things with you?'

'Not so bad, Mrs Chunk. Bit of a ruckus this mornin', weren't it? The cottage flyin' in an' that.'

'It was, Mr Squint. Coulda knocked me down with a feather. I thought my Humpy did good, though. Very professional I thought he was.'

'He was, Mrs Chunk. Did you proud.'

'Mind you, I do think them children should have had a proper breakfast. Bread and water, it don't seem right. I mean, they're still growing.'

'Her ladyship's orders, Mrs Chunk. Can't go against 'em.'

'No,' sighed Mrs Chunk. 'Still. Kids need vegetables.'

'Well, I can't stay here chattin'. I got a poem to deliver.'

'A poem?'

'Yep. From the boss to Miss Fly. I helped him write it.'

'Well, that's very kind of you, Mr Squint. My Humpy's always had trouble with words. Unlucky in love, bad at spellin'. Lovely little eater, though.'

'I know that, Mrs Chunk. By the way, he says he fancies pork chops.'

'He does?' cried Mrs Chunk. 'Then he shall have 'em. They might take a while, though. Tell you what, leave the key in the lock and when I get a minute I'll nip down with a plate o' my apple turnovers. Just to keep him going.'

Jimbo hesitated. Both he and Humperdump had got a bit sloppy with security recently. They took their meals in the kitchen, and the steps up from the dungeon were steep enough without having to mess about with the door every time. Usually they didn't bother and just left it ajar with the key in the lock.

'I ain't supposed to, Mrs Chunk,' said Jimbo doubtfully. 'Not now there's prisoners.'

'Oh, get along with you. Just a couple o' kids. They're shut up in cells, ain't they? And Humpy's down there guardin' 'em. I expect you'd like one o' my turnovers, wouldn't you? Fresh made this morning.'

'I would, Mrs Chunk, I would,' said Jimbo. 'All right, then, I'll leave the key in the door. Don't let nobody else go down, mind.'

''Course I won't,' said Mrs Chunk. 'Oh, and while you're about it, seeing as you're going that way, can you take the cat back up?'

'What cat?'

Mrs Chunk pointed to the chair.

'That cat – oh! It's gone. Funny, it was there a minute ago.'

'There was a cat down here?'

'Yes. One of Miss Fly's, I reckon. Must have got shut out.'

'Ah well,' said Jimbo. 'It'll find its own way back up, I 'spect.'

From his dark, greasy hiding place behind the cooker, Neville watched Jimbo cross the flagstones and vanish through the main door. He almost collided with a footman, who came hurrying in bran-

276

dishing a piece of paper which he presented to Mrs Chunk.

'From Miss Fly,' announced the footman. 'The menu for her ladyship's dinner. Excuse me, I have to go and practise a ballet.'

'Ooh,' said Mrs Chunk. 'Something with an apple in its mouth. That's gonna take a while, I'd better get crackin'. Maisie! Flora! See what we got in the pantry, we got our work cut out!'

Her footsteps bustled away.

Neville saw his chance.

'Clover?' called Wilf.

'Yes?'

'Any ideas yet?'

'No. Just stop asking me, will you? If I think of anything you'll be the first to know.'

'All right,' said Wilf. 'No need to be snippy. I just thought we might come up with a plan if we talked about it.'

'What's the point? We can talk all day and all night and next week and next month, but unless we can get hold of a key . . .'

'Ssssh!' hissed Wilf. 'What's that noise?'

'What?'

'*That* noise. Listen. Can't you hear it?'

Clover listened. Sure enough, she could hear a faint sound. It was a sort of intermittent clinking. In between each clink, there was a short pause.

Clink-pause-clink-pause-clink-pause.

It sounded as though something metallic was being dragged down a flight of steps.

'What is it?' whispered Clover. She stood up and moved forward to the bars. She couldn't see him, but she knew Wilf was there because she could hear him breathing.

'Do you believe in ghosts?' whispered Wilf.

'No. Of course not. Don't be so silly.'

The sound was coming closer. There were no longer any pauses. Just a constant clinking, as though the object was now being dragged over a rough surface.

Clinkclinkclinkclinkclinkclinkclink.

And then . . .

A familiar furry figure came trotting out of the shadows.

'Neville!' gasped Clover. 'Wilf, it's *Neville.*'

It was too. Even more astonishing – from his mouth dangled a large brass key! It hung from a ring which was gripped between his jaws. The key was so long that the end brushed the floor.

With some relief, Neville lowered his head and

dropped the heavy key directly before Wilf's door. He pushed it with his paw and sat back, looking smug.

Wilf stooped, fumbled under the bars and grabbed the key. He stood with it in his hands, turning it over in wonderment.

'I don't get it,' said Wilf. 'Where'd he get this from? Where's he been? How did he know . . .'

'Something's happened to him,' said Clover. 'Look at him. He's . . . different.'

They both stared hard at Neville, who gave a vigorous nod. He then raised his right paw and briskly tapped the side of his head.

'Miaow,' he said brightly.

'Either I'm going mad,' said Wilf, 'or is he – *agreeing* with you?'

Neville gave a frustrated little sigh, lowered his paw and drummed his claws. That was the trouble with humans. They were so slow to catch on.

'Neville?' said Clover slowly.

'Miaow?'

'Can you actually understand what we're saying?'

'Miaow!'

'Does that mean miaow yes or miaow no?' asked Wilf. 'I think we need some sort of code here . . .'

He broke off as the door to the guardroom

crashed open. Hastily, Wilf thrust the key into his pocket. Clover backed away from the bars.

'Are you two talkin' again?' snarled Humperdump. 'I thought I told you to . . . ooh. Hello, pussy cat. What you doin' down 'ere, eh?'

He lowered his huge bulk and tickled Neville behind the ear. Neville arched his back and purred delightedly.

'I bet you're one o' Miss Fly's, ain't you? Well, you shouldn't be down 'ere. She'll be missin' you. She'll be . . . .'

Humperdump stopped. He had suddenly had a vision. A vision of him triumphantly returning the cat to the arms of his frantic beloved, whose gratitude would know no bounds. She would come running down the corridor to meet him and throw herself into his arms.

A romantic poem and a successfully returned cat all in one morning. How could she resist?

Chapter Twenty-Five

Escape from the Castle

'Mum?' said Humperdump, bursting into the kitchens. He was panting heavily and had his arms full of Neville.

'Humpy!' cried Mrs Chunk, clattering around the stove. 'Sit down, I'll do your chops as soon as I've got a minute.'

'It ain't that, Mum. I gotta go somewhere. Where's

the key?'

'Ain't it in the door? Mr Squint said he'd left it.'

'Well, it ain't there. I got unattended prisoners down there, I'm s'posed to lock it.'

'He must 'ave taken it with him,' said Mrs Chunk comfortably. 'Calm down, son, I'll keep an eye open. Oh.' She paused. 'I see you got that funny old cat. He was in here earlier, beggin' for scraps. I wondered where he went.'

'Wandered down to the dungeons,' said Humperdump. 'I'm personally takin' him up to Miss Fly.'

'There's a good boy. She'll be pleased.'

'That's what I'm hopin', Mum. That's what I'm hopin'.'

Back down in the dungeons, Wilf was having trouble with the key. He couldn't see what he was doing. The heavy padlock faced outwards and he had to thread his big, clumsy hands through the bar.

'He winked,' said Clover. 'Over Chunk's shoulder, he *winked* at us.'

'I know,' said Wilf. 'I saw. Oh, blast!'

His fingers lost their grip and the key fell to the floor outside the cell. He dropped to his knees and tried to reach it under the bars.

'You know what's happened, don't you?' went on Clover.

'Of course I do. Ouch, the skin's coming off my *arm* . . .'

'You don't, though, do you?'

'Ah, got it, I'll try again. What?'

'You don't know why Neville's gone all brainy. I do. I've worked it out.'

'All right, so tell me. Why is Neville brainy?'

'Didn't you notice? He smelled of aniseed. He's taken the Changeme Serum. He must have been hiding in the cottage and found the bottle. Maybe it broke and he lapped it off the floor. That means he's got an hour's worth of intelligence, if it works the same on cats as it does on humans.'

'Cripes!' said Wilf. 'I do believe you're right. That's not much time. I wonder how long it's been since he took it?'

'Who knows? Anyway, he's obviously worked out some sort of rescue plan. Hurry up before he goes back to normal and forgets it.'

'I'm trying, I'm trying! It's the angle! Oh, blast, dropped it *again*!'

'You'd think he'd have had enough sense to give the key to me, not you. All that intelligence and he gives the key to the clumsy one. You'd think he'd –'

'Clover,' said Wilf firmly. 'I would *really* like you to stop talking now.'

Jimbo Squint stood outside Miss Fly's door. He was getting tired of all this note delivering. There were an awful lot of steps to climb. He hoped this would be the last time.

Briskly, he rapped on the door.

There came a wailing from within, a cry of 'All right, darlings, let Bubby *through*' and the sound of slapping footsteps. The door opened and Miss Fly peered out. Cats seethed around her ankles, purring and yowling.

'Yes?' she said shortly. 'What?'

'Got somethin' for you, Miss Fly,' said Jimbo, holding out the note.

Miss Fly blushed scarlet, groped for a hanky and said, 'I don't want it.'

'You might,' said Jimbo. 'It's better than the others. Anyway, I got to wait for a reply.'

Miss Fly shot out a hand, snatched the note and brought it up close to her pink-rimmed eyes. Her lips tightened as she read it.

'You see?' said Jimbo. 'Poetry. What's the reply?'

'This,' said Miss Fly. Slowly and deliberately, she ripped the note in half. Then in quarters. Four pieces of paper fluttered to the floor.

'You don't like him then,' said Jimbo.

'No!' screamed Miss Fly. 'No, I do *not*! Tell hib to *leave be alone*!'

Humperdump toiled up the steps that led to his beloved's room. He was gasping for breath and bathed in sweat. It was a long, steep climb from the dungeons to the upper levels, which is why he always sent Jimbo. He hoped it would be worth the effort.

Neville had clawed his way up to his favourite position – draped across the shoulders. He was feeling very pleased with himself. So far, everything had gone according to plan. Get Revenge On Booboo – tick. Explore Castle – tick. Have Breakfast – tick. Steal Key From Lock (which hadn't been easy because of cat limitations such as lack of opposable thumbs but problem eventually overcome with help of new-found intelligence) – tick. Take Key To Children – tick. Now all that was left was Create Diversion.

Neville was looking forward to that.

'Done it!'

There was a squeal and the padlock was finally open. Wilf pushed on the bars and the door swung open, sending him sprawling on his knees in the passageway.

'Hurry *up*,' fretted Clover as he picked himself up and approached her cell, triumphantly waving the key.

'I'm *doing* it,' said Wilf, inserting it upside down into the lock. 'These locks are rusty, you know, it's not easy.'

'The other way up. Honestly!'

'I can see, I can *see*. Ah! That's it!'

Finally, the key turned. Clover pushed on the door, which crashed into Wilf, sending him staggering back against the far wall, knocking one of the torches to the ground. Clover snatched it up, held it aloft and stared down the dim passageway. At the far end, a flight of steps curved upwards into darkness.

'Right,' said Clover. 'This is it. Are you ready?'

'Ready as I ever will be.'

'Then let's get out of here!'

Miss Fly was clearly not a poetry lover. Not only had she torn up Humperdump's love note, she was now grinding the pieces under her heel.

'I will not *have* it!' she was shouting in a high, trembling voice. 'I will *not* be pestered in this way . . .'

She broke off. Her eyes widened as she looked

beyond Jimbo's shoulder. A huge, red-faced, panting figure had emerged from the top of the stairway. He was holding out a cat. A strange black cat with yellow eyes. It just hung there, back legs and tail dangling, showing no signs of distress. It didn't look bothered at all.

'Here he is, tell 'im yerself,' said Jimbo sulkily, and turned on his heel.

'Where you goin' now, Jimbo?' enquired Humperdump, as he scuttled past.

'Back down to the dungeons. Don't get yer ear chewed off there.'

'Where's the key? Mum said you got it.'

'I ain't got it. I left it in the lock . . .'

'*What*,' squawked Miss Fly suddenly, 'are you *doing* here, Chunk?'

'Miss Fly,' wheezed Humperdump. He lumbered across the landing and wobbled to a halt. 'It's all right, you can stop frettin'. I've found 'im.'

'What?'

'The cat. Look.' Humperdump held out Neville as though he were presenting a bunch of beautiful flowers. 'I knowed you'd be missin' 'im, so I brought 'im back.'

'What are you *talking* about!' cried Miss Fly. 'That's not one of *by* cats. I've never seen this cat in by life.'

'Eh?'

'These are *by* cats,' shrieked Miss Fly, pointing at her ankles, which were rapidly becoming submerged in a rising tide. More and more cats were squeezing through the doorway, curious to see what all the fuss was about. Some of them had spotted Neville and were beginning to growl. The big tortoiseshell was hissing. Tails were beginning to swish.

Oh-ho, thought Neville. Think you're hard, eh? Right. Time to stop hanging, I think.

And with no more ado, he sank his teeth into Humperdump's meaty hand.

Clover and Wilf came pounding up the dungeon steps. They stepped through an archway and found themselves in a deserted stone corridor, lit here and there by candles placed in niches in the walls.

'Which way to the courtyard?' gasped Wilf. 'Do you remember?'

'To the right, I think.'

'I thought it was left.'

'No, I'm positive it's right. Come on.'

'Just let me check,' said Wilf. 'I'll only go a little way. Just along to the corner. Wait there.'

He sprinted along the corridor. Clover saw him peering cautiously around the corner. He clapped a hand to his mouth and came hurrying back.

'You're right,' he said. 'That way leads to the kitchens. The door's ajar. There's people in there working.'

'Told you,' said Clover. 'It's this way. Give me the key.'

'What? Why?'

'Because there are five other doors. I counted when we came in. And the big gates leading into the courtyard. We'll be all day if you muck about like last time.'

'Well, thanks.'

'Don't look so cross. You can hold the torch.'

'That's not much of a job. Anyway, it's gone out. It's not a torch, it's just a big charred stick.'

'Right. If we run into anybody, whack 'em with it.'

Mesmeranza was standing before her wardrobe debating what to wear for the portrait when she heard the noise.

It was a terrible, ear-splitting howling. It set the teeth on edge. Intermingled with the howling were raised voices and a single, piercing scream.

Mesmeranza strode to the door and wrenched it open. Her eyes widened in disbelief.

Outside her room was a heaving sea of panicked cats!

Some were trying to wriggle under the rug. One was halfway up a wall hanging and another was dangling from the chandelier. Another had leaped into the open visor of a suit of armour and was peering out with hollow eyes. A small ginger was honking up a fur ball under a small side table.

Neville came streaking down the stairs, fur on end and eyes like twin moons. He had always prided himself on holding his own in a fight, but his new brain made him an unstoppable force of nature. Brute force plus *tactics,* no less. He was invincible!

He could herd! He could confuse! He could divide, section off, send them diving for cover, whack them round the ears, drive them dithering into corners or send them swarming up the walls!

Miss Fly's cats, on the other hand, had no such advantage. They were just cats. They slept on her bed. They were spoilt. They couldn't cope with the demon that had suddenly landed in their midst, running at them in a *knowing* sort of way, driving them out of their room and down the stairs and making them all scared and befuddled. They were very vocal in their protests. The noise was deafening.

'Stop it!' came a shrill squeal from on high. 'Oh stop it, you naughty *beast!*'

Miss Fly came slapping down the stairs, shedding hankies.

'Fly?' shrieked Mesmeranza. 'What the devil is going on here? Get your beastly mogs back where they belong!'

She stuck out her foot to try to prevent the cats from entering her room – but to no avail. Sensing temporary sanctuary, they simply skittered past her ankles. Some of them shot under the bed. Three small kittens made for the curtains, swarmed up and hung there, squeaking.

'Get *down*, you little wretches, those are *silk*!'

Mesmeranza strode across to the window and plucked them off. She was about to turn away – when something in the courtyard caught her eye.

Chapter Twenty-Six

I've Got a Big Charred Stick

Stan the sentry was roused from a deep slumber by the sound of running footsteps. He started, snorted and rubbed his bleary eyes. He had been asleep for ages. Nobody had come to relieve him and nobody was looking so in the end he had just sat down on the doorstep and nodded off.

And now, just when he was feeling all muzzy and

crumpled, he was required to leap into action because – wouldn't you just know it? *The prisoners had escaped!* They were racing towards him across the courtyard. One of them – the boy with the red hair – was waving a big charred stick.

Stan struggled to his feet. Where was his pike?

There it was, leaning against the door. He grabbed it and pointed it at the prisoners, who were nearly on him.

'Halt!' said Stan. 'Who goes there?'

'We do,' said the boy. 'Out of the way, we're going in.'

'I don't *think* so,' said Stan nervously.

'Give me one good reason why not,' said the boy.

'Um – I've got a pike?'

'Ah, but I've got a big charred stick.'

'You're holding your pike the wrong way round,' said the girl, pointing. 'Try the pointy end.'

Uncertainly, Stan looked down to check. The boy stepped sideways. There was a sharp pain at the back of Stan's knees and his legs buckled beneath him. His pike clattered to the ground. His helmet fell off and rolled away.

'See?' said Wilf. 'The stick wins.' And he stepped over Stan, pushed open the cottage door and went in.

'You should be careful with pikes,' scolded Clover.

'I'll take this before you hurt yourself.'

She snatched up the pike and followed Wilf. The door slammed shut and there was the sound of bolts being shot across.

At the same moment, a window flew open in a high tower. From somewhere in the background came the distinct sound of yowling cats.

'*Guard!*' shrieked Mesmeranza. 'Get *up*, you fool! *Stop them!*'

Inside the cottage, Clover sprinted towards the private cupboard.

'I'll summon Bernard,' she said. 'You fend off the idiot.'

There was a thunderous knocking at the door.

'Oi!' came Stan's desperate voice. 'Oi, come out! You're not allowed!'

There came the sound of footsteps and Stan's anxious face appeared at the shattered kitchen window.

'Get back!' roared Wilf, advancing on the window, wildly waving his stick. 'I'm warning you!'

'Give me my pike,' said Stan.

'No!'

'Go on,' pleaded Stan. 'It's embarrassing.'

He glanced over his shoulder. People were beginning to arrive in the courtyard to see what all the fuss was about. He was very aware that he didn't look good. He placed a hand on the window sill. Wilf brought the stick down hard on his knuckles. Stan reeled back with his fist in his mouth.

'What's happening, Clover?' shouted Wilf.

'I'm looking for the manual! I can't see it!'

'Can't you remember the words?'

'No! Oh, where *is* it?'

'Well, you'd better hurry up, because we've got company!'

And indeed they had. More people were pouring into the courtyard. Everyone was pointing and shouting. The captain of the guard came racing up. The courtyard was slick with rain, and his polished boots slipped from under him. He went into a long slide, colliding with one of the maids, who fell over with a surprised little scream, knocking over a boot-boy on her way down.

And then . . .

The main door of the castle burst open, and out streamed a stampede of panic-stricken cats! They flowed down the steps and spread out over the courtyard, howling and spitting and getting under everyone's feet. In their wake came Miss Fly, wringing her hands and wailing their names.

'Fluffy! Spot! Oliver! Tibbikins! Cub to Bubby. Oh

cub to Bubby, *do*!'

Humperdump emerged next, sucking his bitten hand. He lumbered down the steps, still hoping to redeem himself in the eyes of his beloved although he had a feeling that things had gone beyond the point of no return.

'Don't you worry, Miss Fly!' he shouted. 'I'll help you! We'll get 'em! Humpy'll help!'

Miss Fly turned on him like a spitting cobra.

'Oh – get away frob be, you stupid, *stupid* ban!' she screamed, and stamped hard on his foot. Humperdump staggered backwards, tripped over the small ginger who was crouched on the step coughing up yet another fur ball, and went down like a stone, bringing two footmen with him.

'Clover!' warned Wilf again. The captain of the guard had picked himself up and was hopping around, trying to untangle his sword which had become caught up in his legs. 'It's getting kind of critical.'

'Ah! Found it!' cried Clover, pouncing on the book, which had fallen under the kitchen table.

Stan was hesitantly approaching the window again.

'Still want your pike?' asked Wilf.

'Yes,' said Stan. 'I do.'

'Here it is, then,' said Wilf, poking it through the window and making threatening little jabs. 'Mind how you take it, it's sharp.'

'*Imp-et-us I lack and need the bubble* . . .' gabbled Clover.

And now, the worst possible thing happened. Mesmeranza appeared in the castle doorway. She raised an arm and pointed a red talon at the cottage.

'Get those children out!' screeched Mesmeranza. 'Get them out *now!*'

'*Arise and bring the sack or you're in trouble!*'

There was a brilliant flash, and the kitchen was filled with coiling green smoke.

'*Now* what?' snarled Bernard from his customary place on the middle shelf. 'I hope this won't take long. I'm in the middle of the crossword.'

'Bernard,' said Clover, 'this is an emergency. We have to take off *right now.*'

'Yes!' howled Wilf from the window. 'For crying out loud, hurry up!'

He and Stan were engaged in a strange dancing ritual with the pike. Wilf kept making little thrusting movements and Stan kept trying to grab it from the side. From outside, there came shouts, cries and yowling noises. Miss Fly was running around in circles, desperately trying to round up the milling cats.

Mesmeranza was striding across the courtyard, kicking everyone and everything out of her way.

'Fly!' she was screaming. 'The Wand! Fetch me the *Wand*!'

'Anyone know the name of a four-legged animal beginning with H?' enquired Bernard, slowly opening the sack. 'Four across. Five letters, ends with an E . . .'

Clover snatched a fork from the floor and advanced on him.

'I said *now*,' she said.

'All right, all right,' said Bernard hastily. 'Keep your hair on.'

From outside came the noise of running footsteps.

'*Quick!*' bellowed Wilf. Stan had finally succeeded in catching the pike, and they were engaged in a desperate tug o' war through the window. The captain was running towards them, sword drawn, and Mesmeranza was bearing down. It was hopeless. Any second now the cottage would be surrounded and it would all be over.

And then . . . And then . . .

They went up.

It wasn't a bit like the first time. There were no creepers to hold them down. There was no jerking or grinding or bucking of floors. The cottage just rose, smoothly and steadily, with no fuss at all. Wilf let go of the pike and hastily backed away from the window.

'Wait!' shouted Clover. 'Stop right there! What about Neville? We can't leave without him!'

Bernard gave an irritable sigh. He made a little adjustment to the bubble that floated between his hands and the cottage paused in its ascent.

Clover ran to the window and peered out, anxiously scanning the courtyard below, where confusion still reigned. People and cats were staring up, pointing in horror at the cottage hovering directly above their heads. In the middle of it all stood Mesmeranza, staring up, face incandescent with rage.

'I'll get you!' she was screaming. 'I'll get you, Clover Twig, just see if I don't!'

'Neville!' bellowed Clover. 'Where are you?'

Down below, Neville sat in the courtyard, looking around in puzzlement. For some reason, there were a lot of cats and humans running around screaming, but he couldn't remember why. Was it anything to do with him? He thought perhaps it might be, but he wasn't sure.

Oh well. He didn't much like this place. It was raining a bit and he didn't like rain. Perhaps it was time to go home.

The trouble was, for some peculiar reason, home was now floating way above his head. He would need a bit of help to get up. That new girl was leaning out of the window, shouting his name. Good. It must be supper time.

Neville's eyes fell on a tall woman standing in the very centre of the courtyard. She had her back to him and was waving her fist and screeching. She seemed to be upset about something. Why? He didn't know. What was her name again? He couldn't remember. But he knew he didn't like her.

She'd do.

Neville took a flying leap and landed in the middle of the tall woman's back. Ignoring her screams and using his claws as grappling hooks, he scrambled up to her shoulder and then on to her head. He tensed, sprang, soared through the air and landed with a thump on the cottage window sill.

'Here he is,' cried Wilf. 'Good old Nev! In you come, boy, we're going home.'

And Neville dropped down into his own kitchen and looked around for something to eat.

'Can I proceed?' enquired Bernard poisonously. 'Or is there something else you've forgotten?'

'Go!' said Clover. 'Go up! Now!'

And up they went. Up past the high grey walls and turrets. Up, up, up over the mountains, up into the lowering skies. Far below, tiny little specks scurried like ants around the fast receding courtyard.

And then they were in the clouds. Wispy tendrils floated by the window, becoming thicker and more dense, then finally blotting out everything. Slowly, the green smoke was dispersing out of the windows.

They'd made it!

Chapter Twenty-Seven

Flying Home

'We've made it,' croaked Wilf. He was curled up on the floor with his head in his hands. 'We have, haven't we? Tell me we've made it!'

'I think so,' said Clover. She stood by the broken window, staring out at the grey cloud, waiting for her heart to steady. Far below, the mountains were a blue blur. Already, the castle was far behind.

'I really thought we'd had it.'

'Me too. I've never been so scared in my life.'

'Did you see me with the pike?'

'I did. You did a great job.'

'So did you.'

'Thanks. But it was mostly all down to Neville.'

They both looked at Neville. He was staring in bewilderment at the place where his basket should be but wasn't. It was upside down in a corner, but he seemed to be having trouble getting his head around this.

'Nev?' said Wilf. 'Are you all right? One miaow for yes, two for no.'

Neville carried on staring into basketless space.

'I think the serum's worn off,' said Clover. 'He's gone back to being his stupid old self again.'

'That's a shame,' said Wilf. 'I was looking forward to finding out all about his adventures. But I guess we'll never know.'

'I do wish you'd stop your endless yakking,' remarked Bernard from the cupboard. 'I'm attempting to keep us steady.'

'You do that, Bernard,' said Wilf. 'It must be really hard, what you're doing. I mean, Clover and I have only spent an entire night and day escaping from dungeons and fighting off guards with pikes. But you, you've got it real tough, sitting in a cupboard keeping a little floating bubble suspended . . .'

'*A horse!*'

The sudden cry came from the window.

'What?' said Wilf.

'It's a *horse!*'

'That's it!' exclaimed Bernard. 'Five letters, beginning with H and ending with E. Why didn't I think of that?'

'No!' Clover was pointing out of the window. 'I mean there's one behind us! A *flying horse!* Oh, Wilf! It's her! She's coming after us!'

Wilf shot up and ran to join her.

Some way behind – but gaining fast – was a tiny, enraged figure. She was riding bareback on a black, snorting horse that sported a large pair of flapping, feathery wings! There had been no time for harness or Special Saddle. Booboo was visible to all and it was an unsettling sight. Finding a mouse in his food had upset him badly and he still had the jitters. He didn't want to go on a ride at short notice and he wanted to make that *very* clear. His eyes were rolling, his legs were a blur and it was all Mesmeranza could do to stay on.

'Faster!' shouted Clover over her shoulder. 'We've got to go faster! She's catching up! She's got the Wand!'

'I can't,' said Bernard. 'It's too dangerous, the

walls won't stand it.'

From outside came a shriek of rage. Mesmeranza had almost drawn level with the cottage. She hauled on Booboo's flying mane and he reared and he lashed at the air with his hooves. She pointed the Wand at the window. Wilf and Clover ducked as a stream of green light zoomed over their heads and fizzed across the kitchen, taking out a large chunk of wall and scattering Bernard with plaster dust.

'All right!' said Bernard hastily. 'I'll try going into emergency overdrive. Just don't blame me if it all goes wrong.'

And with that, he took his little green hands away from the bubble – and blew. Instantly, the bubble shot up towards the ceiling – and began to spin.

From all around came a trembling. The floor vibrated beneath their feet and the walls were beginning to crack. From above their heads came a splintering noise. One of the rafters was starting to buckle.

The most frightening thing of all, though, was what was happening outside. The clouds were speeding up. They raced across the sky at impossible speed. For a split second a rainbow appeared, then vanished again. A heavy squall of rain blew through the window, followed by snowflakes, then hail, then a dazzling flash of sunlight, then forked lightning, followed by a howling wind. It was as though all the weather in the world was happening at once.

Wilf dived beneath the kitchen table, dragging Clover with him. Neville continued to sit right where he was, pondering the mystery of his basket until Clover's hand shot out, grabbed him by the scruff of the neck and hauled him to safety. With a terrible groaning noise, the beam gave way and fell down with a crash, bringing a large section of ceiling with it.

The air was filled with dust and debris, setting them choking and spluttering. The fallen beam lay partly on the floor and partly on the table. The noise was terrible – plates, cups, saucepans, everything was vibrating.

'Arrrrrgh!' howled Wilf. He felt sure his teeth were coming loose.

'Eeeek!' screamed Clover, clapping her hands to her ears.

'Forest coming up!' came Bernard's voice. 'Descending now, prepare for landing! Mind your heads, there might be a bit of a . . .'

CRASH!

Anyone walking in the woods would have had a

terrible shock. One minute there was nothing but a ruined garden with a gate lying on its side and a great big cottage-shaped hole in the middle. The next minute there was a whistling noise, the sound of breaking branches, a rain of falling leaves and finally, an earth-shattering thump . . .

And there was the cottage. Or what was left of it.

It gave what sounded like a huge, juddering sigh. Then . . . slowly . . . it shifted on its base and eased itself down into the ground. There was a pause. A long, long pause, where nothing happened. And then the back door fell off its hinges.

Clover and Wilf stood in the doorway, looking out in grim dismay at a sea of destruction. The garden had already been pretty well decimated by the take-off – but the touchdown had completed the job. The cherry tree now lay on its side, roots ripped from the soil. The lawn was awash with pink petals and broken branches. The little bird feeder that had once hung from the bottom branch was in splinters.

'Aren't you going to thank me?' came a petulant voice from behind. Bernard was standing in the cupboard, bubble back in the sack, clearly ready to go.

'Thanks, Bernard,' said Clover absently.

'Yeah, thanks,' said Wilf.

'And that's the best you can do? You've no idea of

the risks involved, doing what I just did. The skill, the technical difficulties, the –'

He broke off. There was no point in continuing. He was talking to himself.

'Typical,' snapped Bernard, and vanished.

Outside in the garden, Clover and Wilf stood together, surveying the fallen cherry tree.

'Oh dear,' said Wilf. 'That's torn it.'

'She's not going to be pleased about this,' said Clover. 'She was fond of that tree.'

'I was,' said a grim voice from behind them. 'Didn't expect to see it lyin' all over the garden, that's fer sure.'

They both whirled round. Mrs Eckles was standing by the wrecked flower bed, peering down at her feet.

'Mrs Eckles!' gulped Clover. 'I thought you weren't back 'til tomorrow.'

'Yes, well, I came 'ome early. Looks like them crocuses is done for. See? All squashed. Shame, they was a nice colour too. Oooh.' A smile creased her cheeks. 'There's my boy!'

Neville came trotting up, tail erect, and rubbed around her ankles. Mrs Eckles stooped down and gathered him up. He scrambled up to his usual place, draped across her shoulders.

'Ahh,' said Mrs Eckles, tickling his chin. 'He loves his mother.'

Clover and Wilf exchanged a startled glance. Considering the circumstances, she seemed to be strangely calm.

'You've probably gathered that we had a bit of trouble,' said Clover.

'Well, yes.' Mrs Eckles turned and surveyed the wrecked cottage. 'Place has taken a bashin'. I can see that. Take a bit o' fixin' that will.'

'We're really sorry,' said Wilf.

'And so you should be,' said Mrs Eckles sternly. 'Especially you, Clover, I thought you had more sense. You 'ad no business pokin' around in me private cupboard.'

'That was my fault,' admitted Wilf. 'I took the Changeme Serum and picked the padlock. Clover tried to stop me.'

'Hmm. And then you both went off on a little joyride.'

'It wasn't like that,' said Clover. 'There was nothing joyful about it. I don't think you quite —'

'Bernard bein' awkward?' interrupted Mrs Eckles. 'Spot o' turbulence? Well, serves you right. Serves me right too, I s'pose. I shoulda known better than to leave a couple o' kids alone with a bottle o' serum and a cupboard they ain't allowed to open.' Mrs Eckles' eyes were roaming the garden. 'Just look at the state of that chicken coop. I bet that gave Flo an' Doris a turn. I s'pose they ran off in the forest? I'll 'ave the devil of a job gettin' 'em back.'

She wandered off to inspect the mangled coop.

'She's taking it well,' whispered Wilf. 'I thought she'd be really furious, considering her cottage is demolished.'

'I know. I don't think she's getting the whole picture.'

'Huh?'

'Don't you see? She's got it all wrong. She thinks *we* took the cottage up. She doesn't know it was Mesmeranza. She hasn't a clue what's been happening.'

'I bet she does,' said Wilf. 'Witches know everything, don't they? They *see* things in dreams and tea leaves and – I dunno – mystic runes and stuff. Why else is she back a day early?'

'Let's ask her,' said Clover.

'Ask me what?' enquired Mrs Eckles, wandering back with Neville still slumped over her shoulder.

'Why are you back a day early?'

'It was rainin'. Fayre was a washout. Thought I'd make a dash for it on the broom and leave Archibald to bring the gear 'ome in his own time.'

'You didn't get any mystical signs, then? No premonitions that something *bad* might be happening
back here?'

'No. What are you tryin' to say, Clover? Is there
somethin' I should know?'

'Actually,' said Clover, 'there is. You see . . .'

She didn't get any further.

Chapter Twenty-Eight

The Final Reckoning

A wind came. It came with a rushing roar, whipping the words out of Clover's mouth. The treetops lashed like waves at sea, sending leaves whirling down. And suddenly – with a *whoooomp*! – there was a large flying horse in the garden. Neville scrambled down from his perch and fled under a bush. He didn't like horses. Especially this horse, although he couldn't remember why.

There wasn't a lot of room for Booboo, because of the fallen cherry tree. He was confined to a small-ish space between the tree and the hedge, so rearing and bucking and wing-stretching opportunities were limited. He resigned himself to rolling his eyes, whinnying wildly and attempting to nip his rider on the arm as she dismounted in a flurry of red robes.

'Aaah,' said Mrs Eckles slowly. 'I *see*.'

'I did try to tell you,' said Clover.

Mesmeranza didn't look her best. Her hair was a bird's nest and her face had a curious flattened look from riding into the wind. She had gnawed off all her lipstick. Her green eyes were watering, sending little rivers of black down her cheeks. She looked exceedingly bad-tempered.

'Oh, *drat*!' she snapped, drawing up short and staring at Mrs Eckles. '*You're* here.'

'Yep,' said Mrs Eckles. 'Didn't expect that, did you? Stand back, you two. This is family business.'

Hastily, Clover beckoned Wilf and they both moved back to the edge of the lawn.

The two witches squared up to each other, the trunk of the cherry tree between them. Mesmeranza had the Wand in her hand. Mrs Eckles had nothing.

'Bin a long time,' said Mrs Eckles. 'I see you're still

wearin' daft shoes.'

'It has,' agreed Mesmeranza. 'And just look at you. I don't believe you look a day younger.'

'I take it all this is your doin'?' Mrs Eckles gestured at the chaos surrounding them.

'Yes, as a matter of fact,' said Mesmeranza. 'Didn't I do well?'

'Well, I can see you're pleased with yerself,' said Mrs Eckles, adding, 'O' course, it's easy when you got all that equipment. All Grandmother's old stuff. I see you got the Wand. Used the Poncho of Imperceptibility, did you? I'll bet the Hypnospecs and the Bad Weather Umbrella featured in there somewhere, eh?'

'So? It's up to me what methods I use.'

'Shame you can't do nothin' unless you got all the *gear*.'

'You're just jealous,' snapped Mesmeranza. 'Jealous because Grandmother left it all to me. And now I've got the cottage too. You know the rule. The moment I stepped over the threshold, I made it my own.'

'Yes, and look at it. Just a pile o' rubble. Always was a wrecker, wasn't you? An' after Clover'd got it lookin' so nice an' all.'

'Well, pile of rubble it may be, but it's *my* pile of

rubble. Step aside.'

'I don't think so,' said Mrs Eckles, planting her feet more firmly and folding her arms.

'No?' With a thin smile, Mesmeranza raised the Wand.

'Don't you raise that Wand at me,' said Mrs Eckles, adding threateningly, 'I'll *stare*. *Then* you'll be sorry. Remember what happened when you snatched the spade off me that time?'

'Ah, but I didn't have Grandmother's Wand then . . .'

CRAAAAAAAAAAAAACK!

A massive thunderclap rent the heavens. Booboo reared and let out a mad, panicked neigh as a shaft of lightning forked down, setting fire to a small bush and plunging into the ground next to the fallen cherry tree. Black smoke boiled up from the hole . . .

And there was somebody else in the already over-crowded garden.

It was a tiny, bent, *incredibly* old woman. She was dressed in an old knobbly dressing gown and her feet were stuffed into carpet slippers. Her wild grey hair stuck out from beneath an ancient night cap.

Her eyes were emerald green.

'Crikey,' Wilf whispered to Clover. 'Who's this?'

'I don't know,' said Clover, 'but she certainly

knows how to make an entrance.'

The old woman stared around at the assembled company. She noticed the burning bush, twiddled her fingers, and instantly the fire went out. Her eyes fell on the Wand in Mesmeranza's hand. She pointed a gnarled finger.

'*Drop it! Now!*'

'Oh,' gulped Mesmeranza. The Wand dropped from her fingers.

'And *you*!' The finger pointed at Mrs Eckles. 'Stop the staring!'

Mrs Eckles unfolded her arms and shuffled her feet sheepishly. Together, looking and sounding rather like naughty children, they chorused, 'Hello, Grandmother.'

Wilf and Clover stared at each other in astonishment.

'But I thought she was . . .'

'So did I. Sssh.'

'I'm not staying long,' said the old woman. 'The chiropodist is coming to do my feet.'

Booboo was pawing the ground and making snorting noises. Without even looking, she reached behind her and smacked him smartly on the nose.

'And that's enough from you and all,' she said, and Booboo meekly subsided.

'Well, this *is* a surprise, Grandmother,' said Mesmeranza.

'Yes,' said Grandmother. 'Not a good one, though.'

'Oh, but it *is*. Isn't it, Demelza?'

'Oh, yes,' agreed Mrs Eckles. 'Lovely to see you, Grandmother. How are things in the Twilight Home For Retired Witches? Looking after you, are they?'

'What do you care? You haven't come to see me, either of you.'

'You said you didn't want us to,' objected Mesmeranza. 'We asked about visiting hours and you said you didn't want us showing up with a daft bunch of flowers.'

'True,' said Grandmother. 'I don't like flowers and I can't be bothered with your everlasting squabbling. Couldn't believe it when I saw you were still at it after all this time.'

'*Saw*, Grandmother?' said Mrs Eckles. 'You – er – bin watchin' us, then?'

'Oh yes. They've installed one of those newfangled Communal Scrying Screens in the lounge. We all tune in and take turns watching what our rubbishy relations are up to. Pretty shocking viewing it is too.'

'Er – how *long* have you been watching exactly?' asked Mesmeranza uncomfortably.

'Long enough. I would have left the pair of you to get on with it, but it's all got out of hand, hasn't it? That's why I'm here, even though I'm missing the Bingo. I'm supposed to be *retired,* remember? Do you think I'm in the mood for all this? Look at the state of that cottage!'

'Well, we all know who's to blame for that,' Mrs Eckles put in. 'Nothing wrong with it before *she* tricked her way in. Using all your *things*, Grandmother.'

'So?' Mesmeranza glared. 'A witch takes what she wants by fair means or foul. *You* taught us that, Grandmother. I wanted the cottage, so I took it.'

'Yes, and smashed it up in the process,' said Mrs Eckles tartly.

'Oh, belt up the pair of you,' snapped Grandmother. 'See how quiet those kids are? You want to take a leaf out of their book.'

Her green eyes swivelled to Clover and Wilf, who tried looking even quieter. Old and tiny as she was, there was something very frightening about Grandmother.

'But –' began Mrs Eckles.

'But –' started Mesmeranza.

'I said *enough*!' Grandmother took a large watch out of her dressing gown pocket. 'Look at the time. The tea trolley's due. I can't stay around here. This is what's going to happen. Mesmeranza, you're going to get on Booboo and *go*. I think we've all had quite enough of you for the time being.'

'Oh, so *I'm* the bad one in all this, am I?' cried Mesmeranza.

'Well, yes, obviously. You *want* to be, don't you? That's your style, isn't it?'

'Oh.' Mesmeranza looked thoughtful. 'Yes. Of course it is. I see what you mean.'

'There you go, then. You haven't got your own way this time, but sometimes good wins out over bad. That's life. Get over it. And when you get back you'd better get the castle sorted out. I've seen the terrible state it's in. The next time I tune in I want to see it like I left it. Go on, off you go.'

Everyone watched as Mesmeranza turned and stalked over to Booboo, who unhelpfully backed away. She seized him by the mane and he tried to nip her. She stood on an upturned flowerpot, wobbling on her shoes, and pulled herself astride. Then she glared down and pointed a red talon.

'You wait!' she hissed. 'I'll be back! I may have lost this time, but –'

'Ah, enough with the vengeful speeches,' said Grandmother. 'Just shut up and go. *Up*, Booboo!'

Booboo went up. He took a leap into the air, extended his wings and rose into the dark sky. In seconds, he was a tiny speck – and then he was gone.

A single red high-heeled shoe came hurtling down through the air and fell with a plop on the ground at Mrs Eckles' feet.

'Hah!' said Mrs Eckles. She drew back her foot and kicked it triumphantly over the fence.

'And you can stop looking so smug, Demelza,' said Grandmother. '*You* haven't come out of this looking so smart. You should have run checks on all of those cakes. Thought I'd trained you better than that.'

'I know,' said Mrs Eckles ruefully. 'Sorry, Grandmother.'

'Don't do it again. And take better care of the cottage. Look at the state of it. I hope you're ashamed.'

'I am,' said Mrs Eckles. 'Um – any chance you could give us a quick hand fixin' it? I know how good you are at this sorta thing. Clover an' Wilf'd like to see how it's done, wouldn't you?'

'Yes, please,' chorused Clover and Wilf obediently.

'You can stop sucking up, flattery doesn't work with me. But – well, all right. I'll help you out just this once. You, girl! Pass me my Wand.'

Grandmother pointed to the Wand, which lay abandoned on the ground. Clover ran over and picked it up gingerly. Yes. It was buzzing a bit. Hastily, she placed it in Grandmother's outstretched hand.

'Must say it feels good to have it in my hand again,' said Grandmother thoughtfully. There was something – *dark* in her voice.

'Now then,' said Mrs Eckles rather nervously. 'You're using it for good this time, remember?'

'You're right,' said Grandmother with a little sigh. 'I am. Stand back, away from the tree. Move into a space where you won't get clonked.'

She waved her Wand . . .

And showed them how it was done.

Chapter Twenty-Nine

How It Ends

It was evening. Clover, Wilf and Mrs Eckles sat in the garden, enjoying the last of the sun's rays. The sky was red. A blackbird was singing. It was all very peaceful. They were drinking tea and staring at the cottage.

The cottage stared back – but in a *good* way. It had an air of contentment. It had a new chimney. There was new glass in all the windows. The thatch was thick and yellow. Fresh creepers had twined up, covering the back wall, which was free of cracks. The doorstep had been whitened, and the back door had a coat of smart green paint. The whole thing wasn't slumped to one side. It stood straighter and taller.

The garden was well again too. The cherry tree was back in the ground and awash with pink blossom. The bird feeder hung from the lowest branch. It was stuffed with nuts. The privy was the right way up and the log pile was tidy. Neville lay asleep, snoring contentedly. Flo and Doris were admiring their new coop, which was much smarter than the last one.

'It all looks *so* much better,' said Clover. 'She did an amazing job, didn't she? To do all that in the blink of an eye.'

'Well, yes,' agreed Mrs Eckles. 'We was lucky, though. Could 'ave gone either way. She's mellowed, but you still never know with her. Old habits die hard.'

'It's a shame she just disappeared. She could have stayed for supper.'

'Oh, you wouldn't want 'er for *supper*. You can't trust 'er. She might be retired, but she's still a witch. Notice she pocketed the old Wand? I bet she plays havoc with that at the Twilight Home. They don't allow weapons. I s'pose I'll have to drop in on 'er some time soon. I won't take flowers, though.'

'I'll make some biscuits,' said Clover. 'You can take those.'

They all sipped their tea and carried on admiring the garden, which was bathed in an orange glow.

'The front's just the same,' said Wilf. 'It's a shame she didn't improve that.'

'Why should she? This is a witch's cottage. Like I keep tellin' Clover, it's *supposed* to be frightenin' at the front.'

'But it's still got the same gate. I went and checked. It's gone back to being bad-tempered again. Told me to take my hand off and squashed my fingers.'

'Yeah, well, I'm gonna replace that meself,' said Mrs Eckles. 'Soon as I get round to it.'

Somehow, though, Clover didn't think she would.

'I'm going to go in and start getting supper ready,' said Clover, standing up.

She was looking forward to that. Not only was the cottage improved on the outside, but the inside was immaculate as well. Everything was perfectly clean and tidy. The fallen beam was back in place for Wilf to bang his head on (which he had, of course, the moment he walked in). Everything that had been broken was either mended or replaced. The furniture was back in its proper place and she had noticed a lot of new, interesting food items in the well-stocked larder.

'I'll join you,' said Mrs Eckles. 'It's gettin' chilly. Will you stay for supper, Wilf? I wanna hear all yer adventures in detail. Reckon you an' Clover've got a lot to tell me. I'd like to 'ear both versions.'

'I ought to go home,' said Wilf reluctantly. 'Grampy'll be frantic by now. I've got a lot of explaining to do.'

'I'll drop 'im a note,' said Mrs Eckles. 'I'll remind 'im about 'ow 'e used to come pinchin' me cherries when 'e was a nipper. That'll shut 'im up.'

All three of them walked to the cottage door, with Neville twining around their feet. Wilf tripped over him and dropped his cup on the doorstep. It smashed into pieces.

'Oops. Sorry about that.'

'Leave it,' said Clover. 'I'll see to it later.'

They went in, closing the door behind them. Clover pulled the curtain across the kitchen window. There were cheerful clinking noises and the low sound of conversation. After a while, smoke came out of the chimney.

Out in the garden, the last rays of the sun hit the

very top tips of the cherry tree. And then, slowly, dusk came, bringing owls and night noises. The moon rose and the stars came out. Orange – dark blue – silver.

Wilf came out and went home to face the wrath of Grampy. Somehow, he didn't think Mrs Eckles' note would help. It said: *To ThE ChERRy nikkeR. LEEv the lad alon EE Dun gud.*

A short time later, the door opened a crack. Neville came out and strolled off into the forest.

Later still, Mrs Eckles came out, shut up the chickens and stood for a moment under the cherry tree.

'Hah!' she said. That's all. Just 'Hah!' Then she went back in again. There came the sound of bolts being drawn.

Much, much later, Clover Twig stood at her open bedroom window in her nightie, staring out into the darkness. She was thinking that she would wear her blue dress tomorrow. The green one was more than ready for a wash. She would do that while Mrs Eckles set up a new batch of protection spells. And then, because everything was perfectly clean and tidy, she would take the rest of the day off and visit home. She was sure everyone would have a thousand questions to ask. She would have to be careful how

she answered them. She didn't want to lose the job, after all. It was interesting, keeping house for a witch.

Clover rubbed her eyes, yawning widely. She was just about to draw the curtain and flop into bed, when something caught her eye.

There was a strange object in the sky and it was coming closer. It looked like a box. A square, ordinary box that for some reason was flying!

Skimming the treetops, the box sailed into the garden. It came to a hovering halt over the cherry tree, where it appeared to hesitate for a moment. Then smoothly, silently, it floated down and landed gently on the doorstep. Cautiously, Clover craned forward and looked down.

It was full to the brim with carrots, parsnips and potatoes.

Root vegetables.

Hmm.

Clover shivered, shut the window, drew the curtain firmly closed and got into bed. She would tell Mrs Eckles about the vegetables tomorrow. She blew out the candle, snuggled under the covers, sighed happily and fell fast asleep.

The gate, rather grumpily, called out, 'Goodnight.' But Clover was already in the land of dreams.